The Icy Fire of Deception

short stories

Mike Trial

Published by Compass Flower Press
an imprint of AKA-Publishing
Columbia. Missouri
www.AKA-Publishing.com

Table of Contents

Introduction

Ever since Poe invented it, de Maupassant perfected it, Arthur Conan Doyle immortalized it, and Alfred Hitchcock televised it, the suspense/mystery short story has become one of the most popular forms of literature.

Whether we love the characters or hate them, *we remember them.* Which is more than can be said for the introverted protagonists of far too many mainstream short stories. The suspense / mystery story pulls us quickly along with its narrative drive, sharp motivation, and colorful characters. In the following eight stories you'll meet heroes of varying shades of white, villains not always in black, and characters with consciences every color in between.

Cold Cargo

A 747 is a big airplane, but it's far too small a space for a pilot and copilot who hate each other. Especially when one decides to eliminate the other.

Bill, the chief pilot, muttered something.

"What did you say?" I asked.

"Is the door locked?" he repeated, never taking his eyes off the blood red line of Arctic dawn just becoming visible over the dashboard of the 747.

I reached behind me and felt the latch, "Yes, Bill," I said with mocking sarcasm. "All those imaginary Chinese stowaways back in cargo can't get in."

There are only two people, pilot and co-pilot, on the 747s that fly freight from China to the United States. "Nobody can get in—not even your ex-wife," I added, suppressing a grin.

I hoped he'd shut up for a while, but he didn't.

"Susan's gone, she took everything—the house, my retirement, everything, " he moaned. "I'll be flying forever to pay her." He touched the top of the 747's dashboard.

I fished my key ring out of my pants pocket and started clipping a fingernail.

"I wish you wouldn't do that," he said tightly. I forced my temper down, tossed my key ring on top of my flight bag, and climbed out of my seat, "I'm going back to check cargo and stretch my legs." It didn't need checking, but I couldn't stand any more of Bill's whining. Another hour and we'd be within range of the radio relay station at Barrow and back in touch with the world. It's the isolation of these over-the-pole flights that gets Bill going—for two hours you're out of contact with all radio stations, even the satellites. And for some reason, that isolation works on Bill.

As I left the cockpit, Bill slipped on his oxygen mask. FAA regulations require it. This is to prevent anoxia if there's a slow leak in the pressurized hull of the plane and only one man in the cockpit.

It was cold in the cargo hold, which on a freighter is the entire space behind the cockpit. There are no rows of seats, just aluminum shipping containers full of electronic toys from Shanghai. I stood there in the gloom, thinking.

Two years ago, Bill had been one of the most cheerful guys in the company, nearing retirement, a mentor to me. But all that had changed the day he'd come back from a flight to find a note on the kitchen table from his wife, Susan, saying she had left him.

This is not uncommon. Pilots are away from home four days out of seven which will put a strain on any relationship. Soon after Susan left him, Bill developed a heart condition. I was ready to move up to the captain's position. I could almost feel it. Then He whined to the company president that he needed to stay on, needed the money. The company doctor took pity on him and signed a waiver keeping him on flight status so that he'd have a steady paycheck while he got through the divorce.

I'm working for a real compassionate company, I thought bitterly. They'd promised me the captain's position a year ago. But now with Bill staying on, probably for years, I was stuck in the copilot position with half the pay, and no chance of promotion for the foreseeable future.

They promised me that job, dammit! I jammed my fists into my pockets. So what if Bill needed the money, we all need money. Bill's now-ex-wife Susan was a sharp realtor who'd made good money in the

Seattle housing market, bought their house at auction for cash when the market was down, then fixed it up. And kept the title in her name. The house was on the market at $900,000, but Bill won't see any of that windfall. Susan got around the community property laws by deeding the house to their daughter Melissa just ahead of the divorce.

Now I'm stuck in the cockpit with him for fourteen hours at a stretch, listening to his monologue about how life has screwed him, Susan is a devious bitch, all the standard recent divorcée stuff. It goes on endlessly. With occasional interludes about how angelic their daughter Melissa is.

Melissa's twenty four, a bright young commodities trader, living in Chicago, with a brilliant sense of timing and no compassion, which is what successful market traders need.

"Stupid bastard," I muttered. "He thinks his daughter loves him, but she hates him. He's just too dumb to realize it."

I know she hates him—she told me so one rainy afternoon three months ago, after we'd drunk a bottle of champagne and made love in a suite at the Drake hotel. She also told me about the Seattle house being on the market and that she expected to see the cash real soon. It's Melissa's self-centered, unsentimental clarity I like. That, and her athletic young body.

"And when my dad dies," she told me that afternoon, "I'll split the life insurance with my mother, which should get me over the two million dollar mark. With that, I can buy a partnership in a serious firm."

On my flight back to Anchorage from Chicago, I sat in first class sipping a Bushmill's and thinking. Bill's life insurance was a company perk, like mine. If Bill died, Melissa and her mother would get would get five million dollars.

Five million dollars.

I thought about five million dollars, about the years rolling by while I sat in the cockpit seat, with bovine Bill slumped in the captain's seat. I needed a promotion, I needed to live life more fully, I needed a change. And I'd been thinking about how to do this ever since Bill had turned unlikeable.

I made my way down the narrow space beside the pallets until I located the pallet I'd chalk-marked. I opened the inspection panel and pulled out a little grey compressed gas cylinder. Corruption is widespread at Chinese airports, so getting a guy to fill an oxygen cylinder with carbon monoxide and a ramp worker to slip the cylinder into a box of electronics had only cost me a total of $150.

I took the cylinder out, went back to the on-board oxygen system, unscrewed a reserve bottle, screwed in the gray cylinder and manually switched it over. The flow meter showed normal flow. Carbon monoxide is odorless so Bill would feel nothing but increasing lethargy. I envisioned him staring glumly at the red horizon, his mind on his troubles, his chin sinking slowly down to his chest. After a minute I saw the flow decrease as he slipped into unconsciousness. After flow had dropped to zero I removed the cylinder and put the real oxygen cylinder back and switched the system back to automatic. The flow meter stayed at zero; Bill was dead, all his problems solved.

On the cargo deck, I slipped the grey cylinder back into its hiding place. These pallets would be on a Dallas-bound flight less than thirty minutes after we landed in Anchorage. When they were unpacked in some Texas warehouse, the presence of an small untraceable grey cylinder would go unnoticed.

I checked my watch. In forty minutes we'd be back in radio contact and I could call in an emergency, tell them Bill had suffered a heart attack, and that I had been unable to revive him. I'd land the plane, exhibiting the right amount of grief. After all the paperwork was done, all the questions asked and answered, I'd stop by the dispatch office and ask if I could take a few days off to recover from 'the loss of a friend'. Then I'd catch a flight to Chicago and meet Melissa.

I made my way back up to the flight deck and stood for a moment outside the cockpit door. Now that it was done, I felt a twinge of remorse for Bill, for the solid middle class life that had slipped away from him.

I grinned in the darkness. Well, life would not slip away from me. I was about to make a new life. Starting with a new woman and part of five million dollars.

The door knob wouldn't turn. I tried it again. It wouldn't budge. "Damned crazy bastard locked me out!"

I searched frantically for my key, then realized I'd left it on my flight bag in the cockpit.

I slammed against the door again and again. Tried the knob with all my strength, but nothing would give. After 9/11 all aircraft doors had been refitted to prevent anybody, even a desperate man, from breaking into the cockpit.

The plane flew on toward a blood-red dawn, a dead man at the controls, two hours of fuel left.

Silk Air

In the middle of their vacation, Lea walks out on her husband, David. But he races after her and manages to get a ticket on the flight she booked, never guessing the ultimate destination of this unlucky airliner.

Lea Miles sat at the Silk Air departure gate in the Bangkok Airport, bare feet up on her carry-on bag, sipping Jack Daniel's. Two empty mini-bottles stood on the floor beside her sandals.

She considered the purple sparkle-polish on her toenails. *Needs retouching. Like my life.* She finished off the bourbon, screwed the cap back on, and placed the empty on the floor beside the other two.

"David." Her sigh turned unexpectedly to a cough of a sob. She choked it off, anger rising in her at how she'd let him ruin their vacation. And ruin the last five years of her life.

• • •

When they'd planned this vacation to Thailand, their first vacation in three years, he was agreeable—even eager to go—but when they arrived, he decided he was going to do exactly what he pleased regardless of her feelings. "You plan too much. You take all the spontaneity out of life, Lea."

Lea was still unpacking when he announced that he was off to the casino.

"Now? You can go to a casino in Vegas," she told him. "This is the evening we were going to take the riverboat tour with dinner." She looked at her watch. "In an hour. This is our vacation, let's enjoy it."

He smiled the smile she hated. "That's what I intend to do," he said. "You take the tour. I'm going to the casino." He closed the door and left her sitting in the hotel room alone, watching the sun's red ball sinking into the Bangkok smog.

"Travel halfway around the world, but nothing changes," she muttered. Her anger rose up and she began to pace. "Maybe it's time I changed."

She phoned the concierge desk and asked for a reservation on the next available flight to Hong Kong.

She'd visited her friend Karen in Hong Kong six years ago and had the time of her life. Karen had advised her not to marry David.

Lea nodded at her reflection in the mirrored closet doors, "I'll see Hong Kong instead of Bangkok." She picked up her phone, then put it down. "No, I'll surprise her. If she's out of town, I'll just put myself up at a hotel and relax until she gets back. Let David wonder where I am."

She packed a carry-on and started for the door, then paused, pulled open the desk drawer, and wrote a note on the hotel stationery.

Things have not been right between us for a long time. You tell me I plan too much, so I'm leaving you now, with no plan. After all, who knows how much time we have and I'm not going to waste any more of mine with you.

• • •

In the lobby, the concierge desk was crowded with tourists. Lea pushed through the crowd, saw a ticket envelope with her name on it and scooped it up. "This is mine, thank you."

In the taxi to the airport she noticed it was a Silk Air ticket folder, not Cathay Pacific. The flight number, time, and destination were hand written on the folder in neat English: Silk Air flight 298, departing at 9 P.M. for Penang.

Who cares? It doesn't matter where I am as long as I'm away from David. I'll lie around the pool at a hotel in Penang, for a few days, and then go to Hong Kong.

As the taxi dropped Lea at the departures level, David returned to the hotel room, gift shop flowers in hand, prepared to sweet-talk Lea. He read her note, tossed it and the flowers on the bed, and went directly to the concierge desk.

"Mrs. Lea Richardson?" the Thai man at the desk told him. "Yes, booked on Silk Air flight to Penang. Departs in an hour."

"Sell me a ticket," David said pulling out his platinum card. In a minute he had a ticket, full fare, to Penang. He sprinted to the taxi station, jumped in a cab and told the driver to get him to the airport as quickly as he could.

Lea snapped back to reality from a pleasant daydream of lying around a calm turquoise pool at a Penang hotel. "Boarding all rows, Silk Air flight 298." She got to her feet, shouldered her carry-on and shuffled up to the boarding gate. The gate agent slid her boarding pass under the scanner twice, but nothing happened.

The agent examined the boarding pass. "This is not a Silk Air ticket. This ticket is for the Cathay Pacific flight to Hong Kong."

"The hotel must have made a mistake," Lea said.

"The Cathay Pacific flight leaves in twenty minutes," the Silk Air gate agent told Lea, "You have time. The Cathay Pacific gates are right there." She pointed down the crowded concourse.

Lea thanked her and disappeared into the crowd just as an American man burst through the crowd and thrust his ticket at the Silk Air gate agent.

"Flight 298 to Penang?" he gasped.

"Too late. Flight has already boarded," said the gate agent."

"The plane hasn't pushed back yet," he said.

The senior gate agent stopped tapping keys on her computer, picked up her microphone and said something in Thai to the plane crew. On board, Captain Aaron Li authorized the agent to allow a late boarding. The gate agent opened the jetway door and scanned David's boarding pass. "Seat 12 B."

David ran down the jetway and flopped into his seat.

Made it. Once the fasten seat belt sign goes off I'll wander down the aisle, find Lea, and sweet-talk her one more time. There are probably good bars and casinos in Penang.

• • •

When the aircraft reached cruising altitude, Captain Aaron Li surreptitiously pulled a letter from Heaven's Garden Casino out of his jacket pocket and read it again, " . . . pay immediately your debt of one point two million dollars US, or we will be forced to take further measures."

Captain Li knew very well that "further measures" meant a discreet visit to his wealthy father, who would pay the debt immediately. He put the letter back in his jacket pocket. "I will not live with that shame," he said.

"What did you say?" Copilot Henry Cho asked.

Aaron smiled, "I'll take it for a while. Go stretch your legs."

After Copilot Cho left, Captain Li locked the cockpit door.

• • •

On September 14, 1997, Silk Air flight 298, carrying seventy-two vacationers and a flight crew of four to Penang, Indonesia, from Bangkok, Thailand, crashed. There was no threatening weather, no apparent mechanical failure, no indication of terrorism. Twenty minutes into the flight, the Boeing 737 inexplicably pitched down and flew straight into the ground, impacting at nearly 600 miles per hour, disintegrating the aircraft and everything it carried.

No cause for the crash was ever determined.

Stolen Melody

Steve always wanted to be a rich and famous musician, but never had the talent to make it happen. Until he discovers a few sheets of music that he knows will make him great. The only catch is that no one must ever know he didn't write it. And Steve has a plan to make sure that never happens.

Steve hurried up the sunny Milan street, ignoring the people, the shops, all the happy chatter of Italy. He was fed up with Italy, fed up with this tour of Italy Nancy had talked him into, and fed up with Nancy. Fed up with everything his life had become.

He turned a corner at random, then another, moving uphill, into the older part of the cosmopolitan city. The streets narrowed, a few old people passed, the city quickly reverted to its fifteenth century roots. He walked more slowly now, as his anger subsided.

The winding cobbled street was too narrow for cars. The second-floor windows of houses were ground-level with the next house up the hill.

When he stopped to catch his breath, he felt the silence of the old city. Ancient stone with weathered tile roofs surrounded him. Some of the dark windows were devoid of glass. On impulse, he ducked his head inside one of them. He saw an empty room, long abandoned. Cracked, discolored plaster covered its irregular walls and ceiling. The tour guide had mentioned that even in Milan, one of Italy's most modern cities, some of the ancient houses had sat abandoned for decades. The cost of fitting them with running water and electricity was prohibitive.

Steve lifted himself to the sill, then swung both legs inside. A deep layer of dust covered the floor. Smoke stains covered the walls around a tiny fireplace. An open doorframe led into an empty corridor. He stood in the silence, glad, so glad, to be away from Nancy's endless chatter. *The years go by while I work temp jobs to pay for the house Nancy insisted on buying, her Lexus, this vacation. I could have been, should have been, writing music.*

He picked at the cracked plaster as though seeking an answer hidden in the wall. When he and

Nancy had gotten married, he'd told her, "All I want to do is write and play music." But the years passed, he wrote less and less, and now he wrote none at all. "And I've fallen out of love with Nancy," he said to the empty room. But saying it didn't make his frustration any less.

He tried to stuff a plaster chip he'd picked off the wall back into its crack, failed, flung it across the room. There was some yellowed paper deep in the crack. He pulled out four sheets of thick paper, folded twice. *Italians! Trying to fix plaster cracks by stuffing paper into them. So stupid!*

It was quarto paper, very old. Music paper. He unfolded them on the dusty floor. The inked score lines had been drawn with a pen and ruler. The notes were quick hand-drawn ovals, only the occasional staff—scribbled *glissando* here, there *adagio,* and more than once the notation *tenerezza*—tenderly, sadly.

"This must be at least a hundred years old," Steve muttered. He fingered the paper, old paper, a previous century's paper. "Might be worth a few dollars to some collector."

He thumbed through the sheets looking for a composer's name or the title of the piece, but found nothing. He had not read a score since his university days, but his eyes followed the lines, haltingly at first, then faster as the music came to life in his mind.

How long he crouched there hearing the soundless music, he didn't know. But when he rose and folded the sheets, the melody, full of sorrow and a magical ethereal beauty, stayed in his mind.

He tucked the music under his arm and made his way back out into the alley through the glassless window. The alley was empty. His watch told him the tour bus would depart in only five minutes. He had to get moving. He quickly went down the street the way he'd come. Near the bottom of the steep incline was a sign on the side of an ancient building: *Via Achato*. He turned a corner, then another, and was back in modern Milan. At a newsstand he grabbed two newspapers, tossed down a euro, then folded the music into the papers.

"See anything interesting?" Nancy said as they took their seats on the bus with the other pastel-clad tourists.

"Nah, nothing, just stretching my legs." He took his travel bag off the overhead rack and stuffed his bundle inside.

"Lot of newspapers," Nancy said.

He sat down and closed his eyes, "Thought I'd try

to decipher some Italian while we're here." The bus started up, the video screens came to life, describing their route and next point of interest, but Steve closed his eyes, oblivious to the TVs. The score he'd read continued to play in his head. Music he'd never heard before, music his heart was hungry for. As powerful as it was sorrowful, rich, and moving. He ached to play it, to make it his own, to rearrange it into something more attuned to contemporary audiences, but still retaining it's heartfelt sadness and beauty. He pretended to doze so that Nancy wouldn't point out every sight to him.

• • •

On their second full day back home, Nancy went back to work as usual. Steve sat at the kitchen table drinking coffee and checking his email messages. The temp agency had an assignment for him today. He should have been there an hour ago. Steve deleted the message and sat down at his electric piano. He propped up the old sheets of music and began picking out the melody. It took him all morning to reconfigure a single motif of the music into the form and texture of a pop song. But when he was done, it was beautiful. He copied the electronic file into ProTunes and emailed it to Del, his agent.

He ate lunch out of a can, standing at the kitchen sink. His email now had two increasingly angry messages from the temp agency. And a message on his voicemail: "We are going to stop offering you positions if you do not respond to our calls." Steve deleted the messages and phoned Del.

"Steve, I'm glad you called," Del said sarcastically. "The temp agency has terminated your contract. And by the way, while you were gone, the Erawan restaurant said they didn't want you playing there any more."

"Just because I took a week off to go on vacation with my wife?" Steve snapped, feeling unexpectedly wounded.

"Frankly, they haven't been happy with you for a long time," Del said. "Coming in late, leaving early. They told me to tell you that the Erawan is a Thai-Indian restaurant. They asked you repeatedly not to play 'Volaré.' But you did so anyway."

Del was silent for a moment, then, "Sorry, Steve. I don't have anything else for you. Maybe you should check with LA City College, they're always looking for adjunct faculty to teach music. You'd make a good teacher, and there are lots of bright young kids . . ."

"I don't want to teach a bunch of kids," Steve told Del. "And I don't want to play crap at a restaurant for people who aren't listening anyway. Check your email, Del. I sent you a file a few minutes ago. It's a new tune of mine. Call me back and let me know what you think." He hung up before Del could object.

Steve set his phone on the kitchen counter and poured himself a generous shot of Ballantine's from the bottle he kept under the sink. It wasn't long until his phone buzzed. "It's fabulous, Steve!" Del shouted. "Your trip to Italy must have really inspired you. This is the best work you've done in years!"

Within a week Steve's tune had been downloaded two million times. Suddenly Del could get him bookings all over Los Angeles and Orange County. He was interviewed at KTTV and KHJ and at the USC music center. Del booked him a series of play dates in Northern California and Steve went on the road.

On the road, Nancy and the dingy little house in Reseda were forgotten. Steve loved the adulation he was getting at the clubs where he played. And afterward at the hotel bar, women would approach him and he seldom turned them down. Good looking women, too.

But, soon the tour ended, the limo dropped him at the same old house in Reseda, and the same old

Nancy came home after work. They ate the same food, and watched the same TV shows. Late at night Steve would sometimes stand in the darkened kitchen leaning against the kitchen sink, sipping Johnny Walker Black, while Nancy slept. Thinking about other tunes. Great tunes. He began to spend his nights secluded in the converted bedroom he used as a study.

He released another tune, then went on the road again and when he got back, Del showed him the numbers. He was netting over fifteen thousand dollars a week. But the money was gone as soon as it arrived. Nancy had remodeled the old house, bought clothes. Steve had no interest in anything she'd bought. He just wanted to be rid of this house and this wife. But he suppressed his anger and began working on a new tune. Three weeks later Del had him booked on another tour, this time for two weeks in Vegas.

Steve returned from Vegas flushed with success, expensive whiskey, and beautiful women. He dropped his suitcase in the recarpeted, repainted living room, and went straight to the kitchen, poured out the Johnny Walker, then opened the bottle of Laphroaig whiskey he'd bought on his way to the house. The expensive single malt was smooth on his tongue.

Only then did he notice Nancy's note on the kitchen counter, next to the microwave where she stacked the unpaid bills. It read, *I don't know who you are any more. You're never home and when you are, you're not with me. I can't live like this any longer.*

Steve left it on the kitchen counter while he prowled the house, whiskey in hand, "Screw her!" he said, but when he thought about it, he felt no anger, only a great and glorious sense of relief. *I'm glad she's gone.* He made a mental note to have Del get him an attorney who could get him a divorce quickly and cleanly. Nancy could keep this house. In the meantime he'd let his royalties accumulate in his account at Del's agency where she couldn't touch the money.

• • •

A year later, in his glossy new Marina Del Rey condo, Steve decided to find out something about the four pages of mysterious music that were making him rich. All he remembered was that they came from an abandoned building on a tiny street not far from Via Achato in Milan, Italy. He hired a historical research agency to determine if a famous musician had ever lived in that area. He told them nothing about the music. Two weeks later their report arrived in his email. Guiseppe Verdi had lived in a garret in that part of Milan for a part of 1840. The researchers provided a lengthy biography of Verdi along with a list of the operas he'd written. At the bottom of the list was a note mentioning *Rocester*, "an opera whose score has never been found." In that same year, when he was just beginning to establish himself in the world of opera, his son died, then Marguerite, his wife died. Verdi was devastated.

• • •

Steve envisioned a snowy night in Milan, Verdi sitting alone, crying over his wife's death, and writing music, because that was the only way he knew to express the nearly overwhelming grief he felt. As the snow fell outside his window, he wrote and rewrote, putting all the sorrow and longing into the notes. He thought to make it an opera called *Rocester*. When Spring came, he folded the pages and stuffed them into a crack in the wall of the old garret he was leaving behind. He knew he could never work on that music again without feeling the crushing loss he had suffered through. And with the coming of spring, new music was forming in his head, music that would become *Nabucco*, the opera that would make him world famous.

• • •

Steve had never attended an opera in his life, but decided he would go once, just to see what a Verdi opera was like. Happily, the Los Angeles Opera was doing *Aida*.

Steve bought a ticket and drove to the Dorothy Chandler Pavilion in downtown Los Angeles. As he wandered around the lobby, waiting for the opera to begin, he noticed a glass case displaying a page of Verdi's original *Aida* score. He smiled. The notes were in the same hand as those on the parchment in his desk. *Wonder what an undiscovered Verdi score would be worth?*

The opera bored him out of his mind. He managed to stay in his seat until the first intermission, then left. Downstairs, at Kendall's Brasserie, he ordered a double Laphroaig and sat at the bar telling everyone how great the music was, but that opera was an outmoded art form, the music needed to be modernized.

Back home, he sat down in his big white chair and looked out over the lights of Marina Del Rey, ten floors below. He slipped an Estevez Ermil cigar out of its tube, clipped the end, and lit it. It was a non-smoking building, but Steve had paid the Mexican kid who cleaned the windows to disable the smoke detectors a week after he'd bought his condo.

The smoke was mellow. He put his feet up, sipped the smoky fire of his Laphroaig.

"Thanks, Giuseppe," he toasted his reflection in the glass wall overlooking the marina lights. "You wrote it, I arranged it, we made a fortune. Glad you're not here to help me enjoy the money." It had been a great two years. After his first song had gone platinum, he'd hired a PR agency to screen him from the deluge of producers wanting to handle what MusicMaker was calling "the greatest talent of his generation." He released one new song every six months for three years. And they all went platinum.

Steve poured another shot of Laphroaig and toasted the dozen framed certificates on the wall over the fireplace. He picked up his phone and checked his account balance: twenty million dollars.

Nancy was gone, but he didn't miss her. Just like he didn't miss his joyless gigs at Erawan restaurant, or the old house in Reseda, or his ratty old car.

I have everything I want.

He took out the four quarto sheets of Verdi's music and touched the end of his cigar to the pages, one at a time, and watched the flame devour the hand-inked notes. *I could have sold this for a million dollars. But if I did that, I would no longer be the "greatest talent of my generation," but just another hack composer stealing melodies from the classics. I can spend the rest of my life on tour, playing my greatest hits. I don't need to write another song in my life and I'll still be famous, and I'll still be rich.*

The door chimed and the girl from the escort service came in, looking gorgeous in a Bottega dress of deep purple trimmed in dark green leather. Steve poured her a double shot of the whiskey and set the decanter down on the glass coffee table beside the ashtray full of ashes.

"Burning the map to hidden treasure?" she asked, raising her glass with a smile.

Steve laughed, "You're so right, baby."

Cold Hands

A large sum of cash is missing from the office safe of San Francisco's most stylish plastic surgeon. The police find fingerprints, but they don't belong to any living person.

"Caught you!" Brendan said, as he stepped into Suzanne's office.

She threw an angry look at him. "Don't scare me like that!" She took her purse out of her desk, then came over to Brendan wearing the perfect smile he loved. They hugged, but she wouldn't let him kiss her.

"Don't smear my lipstick. I've got to go back in to the reception for a few minutes, then check the operating room to make sure everything is prepared for the Practicum. Doctor Rosenblum gets nervous about not being prepared."

"I'll come with you," Brendan said, reluctant to let

her go, but she pulled out of his embrace.

"You go downstairs to the bar and have a drink. I'll meet you there in thirty minutes."

His face fell, but he departed. As he did, the other door to Suzanne's office sprang open and a fuming Doctor Rosenblum burst in followed by a man in a tailored suit carrying a slim briefcase. Cindy, the receptionist trailed in too, crying.

"This has got to stop!" Rosenblum snarled at Phil Weinstein, the tax accountant for Rosenblum LLC.

"Twice a year you tell me we can't balance our books, Phil," Rosenblum addressed the man. Suzanne stood there looking poised and confident. "I make over two million dollars a quarter, and we can't seem to account for twenty—or thirty—or fifty grand every once in a while. You're my accountant! Get it fixed!"

He turned to Cindy, "Clients hand the money to you," he said in a threatening tone, "then you give it to me to put in the safe at the end of the day. Or do you sometimes let it sit in your desk overnight?"

"No." Cindy said in a shaky voice.

Suzanne glared at Cindy. "Yes, you do."

"You always blame me," Cindy began blubbering again, "Doctor Rosenblum is busy, he's hard to catch, sometimes he leaves early, I can't…"

"I've warned her about this before," Suzanne told Phil.

Cindy's face got redder. "I didn't do anything wrong!" she whirled and left the room shouting, "I quit!"

Rosenblum seemed taken aback by Cindy's sudden departure. "Well...I guess..."

Phil put his briefcase down and approached Rosenblum, his downturned hands outstretched, patting the air as though calming a skittish horse. "Let's all calm down, shall we, Richard? All reconstructive physicians have cash accountability problems from time to time; it's a common problem in cash businesses. We tried the police last year and that was a waste of time. Maybe Cindy was taking money," Phil said. "If so, frankly, you're better off just forgetting about it. Hire a new receptionist. Your problem may already have solved itself."

Rosenblum took a deep breath, looked at the accountant, "I don't have time for this right now," he said. "I need to get ready for the Practicum," he glanced at his Patek Philippe watch, "I hope this issue is resolved. If not, I want you to solve it, you hear me, Phil?" He turned to Suzanne, "Go check to make sure the operating room is prepared, okay?"

Rosenblum exited abruptly.

Suzanne rolled her eyes at Phil "I've checked it three times already. He worries too much."

Phil picked up his briefcase, "The cash accountability issues may or may not be solved," he said, staring hard at Suzanne, who returned his look evenly.

"Phil," she said, "we called the police last year and ended up wasting a full afternoon. You said it yourself. This is a cash business. Our clients are wealthy. They want their cosmetic surgery kept a deep, dark secret, so they pay cash. They hand the receptionist an envelope with cash. Cindy was probably helping herself to a little off the top. What does it really matter? You've told me yourself Rosenblum takes in over two million dollars a quarter. Fifty grand is petty cash to him."

"That's part of the problem, he treats these little envelopes full of cash like it is petty cash, but if the IRS suspects unreported income," Phil said, stepping past Suzanne into the corridor, "they will insist on an audit."

"You worry too much," she said. "Isn't that what Dr. Rosenblum pays you to do? Keep the books straight and the IRS at bay." Her tone was neutral, but Phil's expression hardened.

"I'm not a detective," he told her sharply. "You're the office manager. You're the one who should take responsibility for seeing to the proper handling of his cash revenue." He started to say more, then thought better of it.

Suzanne turned away, "Were you about to say you suspect me of tampering with the cash?" she asked sweetly. "Don't threaten me. And don't tell me what my job is. Anyway, I don't have time to talk about this any more. I've got to check the operating room, make sure everything is prepared for the practice surgery."

• • •

Phil came into the bar, spotted Brendan, and slid into the booth, uninvited. "I'll take a martini, please," he called to the bartender, "Make it a double. I'm Phil Weinstein, Doctor Rosenblum's tax accountant." He and Brendan shook hands.

"Brendan Carter, Suzanne's fiancé."

"Hope you don't mind me joining you," Phil said. Brendan did, but said nothing.

"Sounded like there was discord in the office," Brendan said. He sipped his Jameson's. "Not long ago, Cindy came bursting out of those elevators over there, crying."

When the Martini arrived Phil took an appreciative drink and set the cold glass on the black paper napkin. "I'm a tax attorney, not a detective."

Brendan let that enigmatic statement lie and idly gazed around the bar at the faux Egyptian gold work, the potted ferns, the polished black marble.

"But if Rosenblum wants me to play detective, I will," Phil continued, toying with his glass. He stabbed Brendan with a look over the top of his glasses. "How much money would you estimate Suzanne spends every year?"

Brendan shook his head in irritation, "Why are you asking me? Ask her."

But despite the off-the-wall nature of the question, Brendan had always been curious about how much money Suzanne made. Maybe Weinstein would tell him. Brendan had observed that Suzanne always seemed to have plenty of cash with her. They ate out almost every meal; the restaurants she chose were often pricey, sometimes exorbitantly so. But she insisted she pay her own way. "I've never been dependent on any man," she'd told him once, which had struck Brendan as a strange pronouncement. Must be some kind of serious insecurity there, he thought. But he didn't argue, dating her was costing him a lot, and if she felt she needed to help pay, that was fine with him.

"Oh, I couldn't guess how much she spends. I'd guess she makes ninety or a hundred thousand a year—plus her bonus." Brendan said in an off-hand manner.

"Rosenblum pays her sixty thousand a year, and her annual bonus the last five years has averaged twenty thousand," Phil said flatly. "That's what she makes. I asked you what you think she spends, and you named a figure much higher." Phil finished his drink. "So what does that tell you?"

Irked at Weinstein's prying tone, Brendan said, "Isn't that information supposed to be confidential? And you're implying she's living beyond her means and supplementing her income by embezzling from Rosenblum. But if you had any evidence you'd have called the police long ago."

"We did call the police long ago. Last year about this time in fact. They couldn't solve it. And they made it clear to Rosenblum that they had murders and rapes to deal with, and couldn't be wasting their time on wealthy surgeons who couldn't keep track of their own money."

"Well, I'm sure you'll get it resolved eventually.

Suzanne never talks about office finances with me. I know nothing."

Phil raised his eyebrows. "Well, money occasionally disappears from Rosenblum's safe. Your fiancé is a suspect as far as I'm concerned."

Brendan's frown deepened. "I don't like that sort of accusation. The safe was checked for fingerprints, I assume?" Brendan asked.

"Yeah. Inconclusive. The push-button lock had fingerprints, but they didn't match anyone the police had any record of. And they were not Rosenblum's or Cindy's. Or Suzanne's."

Brendan snorted. "Then thief is not someone who works in the office. Simple." He pointedly checked his watch. Suzanne should have been there by now.

Phil shook his head, heaved a sigh, and made his way out of the bar.

Brendan waited a while longer, paid the check, and took the elevator back to the tenth floor. At Rosenblum's suite, the glass doors were open and over-confident men in expensive casual clothes stood in clusters expounding learnedly to each other.

Rather than fight his way through the crowd, Brendan decided to wait for Suzanne in her office.

• • •

He'd been crazy in-love with her ever since their first blind date six months ago. Living in Los Angeles made it difficult for them to be together, but somehow that made her seem even more desirable. Brendan flew up to San Francisco on the United Shuttle every Friday night and home to LA every Sunday night. He lived for the weekends.

But occasionally, like today, a business trip would take him to San Francisco during the week, and he'd have a chance to see her. His meeting had wrapped up at three, so instead of rushing to the airport he'd caught a taxi to 450 Sutter Street, Dr. Rosenblum's office, and here he was, waiting.

Brendan knew he'd been taking a chance that Suzanne didn't already have plans for the evening. But that's what love is, right? Taking a chance on someone you really care about. And Brendan was ready to take a chance on Suzanne. He loved her beautiful Japanese features: straight, perfect, black hair, white skin, and beautiful hands. Brendan had never been much of a hand-holder in previous relationships, but he found that reaching across a restaurant table and taking Suzanne's warm hand was intoxicating.

She liked to talk about her work, but not about herself, although he did get her to reveal the basics:

she'd been born in Hawaii, got her nursing degree at the University of Hawaii, then moved to San Francisco and worked her way up to office manager for one of the top cosmetic surgeons in the Bay Area, Dr. Richard Rosenblum.

He guessed she'd grown up poor since she clearly loved spending money now. She had exquisite taste in clothes and jewelry and dressed better that any woman Brendan had ever known.

Just as Brendan was about to go looking for her, Suzanne came in, wearing her fur coat, purse in hand. "Sorry I'm running late," she said. "Those doctors love to talk." She rolled her eyes. "But there's a new restaurant I'm dying to try with my favorite person in the whole world." She took Brendan's arm and pulled him into the corridor.

• • •

At Palomino's, the restaurant of the hour in San Francisco, The maître d' helped Suzanne out of her fur coat to reveal her perfect body in a really fantastic Bottega Veneta red and black dress, a Bulgari necklace of pink and greens stones around her neck.

They were given a choice table with a spectacular view of the Bay Bridge.

"You look great," Brendan said. They sat down

and opened the menus. "Some difficulty in the office today?" he said, just making conversation.

Suzanne closed her menu and looked out the window.

Brendan amended, "I mean…it's none of my business really…but…"

Suzanne said nothing.

"Sorry. Didn't mean to pry."

"Just leave it alone," she said softly. After a minute her smile returned and they ordered dinner. Brendan noted hers was the most expensive item on the menu.

"The office problem is a tempest in a teacup." She laid her hands on top of Brendan's, pushing his fingertips down gently on the linen tablecloth, one by one.

Searching for a different subject, Brendan said, "What's this Practicum Dr. Rosenblum's hosting this evening?"

"Twice a year he hosts a gathering of the more prominent reconstructive surgeons in the Bay Area. A seminar where they share the tricks of the trade. It's a bit of an ego thing. They all want to show off in front of each other. They are a big-ego crowd, these cosmetic surgeons."

"It seems to me they'd want to keep the tricks secret."

"This is for their charity work," Suzanne told him. "Reconstructive surgery, not cosmetic surgery. They are all so proud of donating their time to helping the needy." She laughed. "Gets them some good publicity."

"What's so funny?"

"The 'needy.' " Suzanne said. "The needy who probably make more than you and I put together. Wealthy Marin county people who want their knees fixed after too much jogging and claim it as a job-related injury. It's a Practicum on Carpal Tunnel Syndrome surgery. First there's social hour, where they reassure each other how important this 'charity' work is, and then they step into Rosenblum's surgery and practice what they've been talking about."

"Practice on patients?" Brendan's eyebrows went up.

"Cadavers," Suzanne said. Brendan looked at his steak, thought of dead people's hands, put his utensils down and took a healthy slug of his cabernet.

"Not full cadavers, just wrists and hands," Suzanne went on calmly. "They're all laid out on stainless steel trays in his operating room now, that's what I was checking on. We get them from the research hospital in Oakland. After the surgeons practice their surgery, the remains are burned." She noticed his expression. "Sorry about such a gruesome subject. For nurses and doctors, it's not a big deal."

When the waiter had cleared their plates they both ordered crème brulée and coffee.

Maybe it was the wine, but for no reason at all, Brendan found himself telling Suzanne about his conversation with Phil Weinstein in the bar.

Suzanne laid her spoon down and listened, expressionless. "That bastard!" she said softly. "Suspecting me of stealing cash. And telling you about my salary. That is so unprofessional."

Brendan, wishing he'd never brought it up, quickly tried to backtrack. "Weinstein was just blowing off steam. I guess Rosenblum's putting pressure on him. I told him you should just call the police."

"That's stupid!" Suzanne snapped at Brendan. "Call the police? Really!" she laughed a sarcastic laugh. "Last year we did call the police. Their lab results indicated the safe only had smudged prints of someone they thought might be a vagrant who died two years earlier." She snorted. "They've proved their incompetence. We don't need to go through that again."

Irritated, Brendan came back with, "So someone from outside the office is getting into the safe."

Suzanne stood up, "None of this is any of your business." She put her napkin aside, "I'm going to the restroom."

• • •

Brendan finished his glass of wine and the waiter refilled it.

"This is the worst date we've ever had," he muttered. He stared at traffic streaming up the ramp to the Bay Bridge. Suzanne likes nice things and buys them. He knew he was smitten with her, and he was sure she cared for him. They were beginning to use the 'L' word with each other. Her money and what went on in her office really was none of his business. He should learn to keep his mouth shut.

Suzanne returned to the table trailing a stream of admiring glances from the men at other tables. She was smiling again. Brendan started to apologize but she put her fingers on his lips, "No, let me apologize. This has been a tough day. I lost my temper at Cindy and she quit. But that's okay, we can find another receptionist, and I'm convinced she was taking money, which is what this little flap was about. To you and me it would seem like a lot of money, but to

Rosenblum, it's just petty cash and he doesn't want to be bothered with it. And he's got the combination to his safe written down on a sticky note right on his desk. It probably is someone getting into the office after hours somehow. I don't think Rosenblum cares if building security is lax, or if the receptionist skims money, he's only worried about keeping his wealthy clients happy and keeping the IRS off his back."

Suzanne's tone changed. "But I don't want you asking me about my income. That's impolite. I'll never ask you about yours."

Brendan toyed with his coffee spoon, "Rather rigid rules."

She smiled. "Rules only seem rigid if you don't like them. But I'll never change that, not for you, not for anyone." She softened her tone. "Don't you see, money is not important. I'm not hung-up on it. I like nice things, so I buy them, that's what money is for."

They sat in silence for a moment, then she pushed their coffee cups aside and took his hands, "I didn't mean to ruin our dinner talking about body parts and money." She smiled at him, looking gorgeous. "I do love you, you know."

• • •

"Time for me to go." Brendan told her gently. "The last shuttle back to LA leaves at ten."

At the airport she got out of the car and hugged Brendan hard. "I'll miss you," she told him. "After we get married, we won't have to do this every week."

"Yeah," he breathed. "Let's get married soon. Next month?"

Her smile was radiant, but she got back in her car without a word, then slid the passenger window down.

"We'll talk about it next Friday night," she said.

"I'll be right here at seven," Brendan said.

"It's a date," she said. The window went up and she sped away.

On the plane, Brendan watched the coastline sliding by in darkness and thought about Suzanne, her warm hands in his. His thoughts drifted to body parts, Rosenblum's Practicum, to the missing cash, to Suzanne's expensive tastes. And then he thought about how the operating room must look. Dead hands on stainless steel trays. Suzanne arranging them, laying the hands out in preparation for surgery. He remembered how she had pressed down on his fingers at the restaurant, and that's when it all became clear to him.

He got a Jameson's whiskey from the passing drink cart. Outside in the night, the lights of Santa Barbara flowed past.

He knew he should call the police, tell them how the thefts were committed, be a hero in Rosenblum's eyes, stay in LA, and forget about Suzanne.

But he wasn't thinking of Rosenblum's eyes, he was thinking of Suzanne's. And how good it felt to hear her say she loved him. So what if Suzanne read the combination to Rosenblum's safe off his sticky note, used a cadaver hand to open his safe, helped herself to money that wasn't rightly hers? Nobody was getting hurt. Rosenblum had plenty of money, and so did the women he treated.

Brendan finished his drink, switched off the overhead light and tilted his seat back. He knew he'd be on the plane to San Francisco next Friday evening. And he knew Suzanne would be there to meet him, looking stunning.

Free State

A North Sea storm traps Annifrida on an ancient oil platform with its two full-time tenants, one of whom wants to kill her. There's no way off the platform, so Annifrida must take matters into her own hands.

Through the wind-blown spray, Anni saw Gullveig Station rising out of the North Sea like a titan on concrete legs. Rows of huge gray waves stretched to the horizon. She clutched her seat belt more tightly as the helicopter buffeted down through the storm toward the landing pad on top of the former oil platform. Beside her, the muscles in the pilot's neck were rigid, his beefy arms knotted, wrestling the helicopter's controls in the gale. "I touch down and you go. Too much wind to land," Evald shouted.

An hour ago it had seemed like a good idea to go the station ahead of the storm, but now...

Anni had talked Operations Manager Karlstrom into authorizing a trip to Gullveig Station despite the gale. And she had flirted with Evald, the Norge Avia pilot, until he'd agreed to fly out to the station ahead of the storm. She reminded him he could file a flight plan that would get her to the station just ahead of the storm, then, with all the airports in southwestern Norway closed, keep going west. Ride the sixty knot tailwind to Aberdeen Field Airport in Scotland. Sit out the storm in the Aberdeen pubs.

The weather service operator looked at the flight plan, looked at Anni and Evald, "In two hours the whole North Sea will be sixty knot winds, ten meter waves."

Anni and Evald exchanged glances, Anni grinned at the weather service operator. He sighed, stamped his approval on the flight plan, then added, "You are crazy, Annifrida. And you, Evald..." He snorted, tossed the flight plan back to Evald, and stomped off.

Anni breathed a silent sigh of relief. She had to get to the station today, had to talk to Bengt Borreson. He was getting too close to finding out her little secret.

• • •

This wasn't the first time Anni had flirted the Norge Avia pilots into flying her out to Gullveig Station on request. Nobody at Nordstaatenergie cared much about the relic that Gullveig Station had become, so when she made her maintenance visits really didn't matter. She'd been using her looks to get her way with men ever since her Japanese father had left her Norwegian mother when Anni was sixteen.

Her father hadn't left Anni much, but her Japanese eyes with her mother's blonde hair, which Anni kept buzz-cut short, tended to turn men's heads.

Swathed in company coveralls and parka she and Evald climbed into the helicopter already rocking in the rising wind. Anni knew Evald's love of single malt whiskeys. Waiting out the storm at the pubs in Aberdeen would be just fine with him.

But now, as they approached the station, jolting through the swirling air toward the postage stamp sized landing platform, it didn't seem like such a great idea. If they went down, there would be no chance of rescue.

Anni didn't have a choice; her secret would be discovered within days. She cinched her four-point seat belt tight. She'd made a hundred thousand euros scamming the company over the course of the last two years using a little vampire program she'd implanted in the station's ancient power management system. And she'd spent all the money. It hadn't been hard to get accustomed to a new car every year and the two-bedroom flat she was now renting, and her annual two weeks in Bali.

But now somebody else was in the system, somebody on Gullveig Station, doing the same thing she was, only far less elegantly. They were manually changing phase to artificially put delivered power efficiency down, mismatched slightly with demand, while short-selling NSE shares on the Geneva Bourse as wholesale megawatt prices fluctuated accordingly.

It originated at the station, so it had to be Bengt Borreson. She had tracers in her software to warn her if company quality control or the North Europe power distribution commission was monitoring her moves. It wasn't them.

Bengt's ham-fisted manual manipulation was so amateurish; Anni had had to work quickly to cover it up so that company quality control monitors hadn't noticed.

She needed to convince him, immediately, to quit doing that. She was willing to cut him in for a part of her profits, if he'd keep his hands off the system.

They could both make money.

• • •

Gullveig Station's radio towers had rusted away and fallen into the sea years ago. Now the top of the station was a simple landing platform with a steel box at one corner, which was the top of the enclosed stairwell down into the station. She had a glimpse of the door standing open, latched back against the howling wind, and then the helicopter jolted down onto the deck. One wheel hit hard. The helicopter skittered and began to rise. Evald shouted a curse and motioned with his head. Anni detached her seat belt, popped her door open and jumped out onto the deck clutching her valise to her torso with both arms. She lost her footing and fell flat, which saved her life as the downwash from the rising helicopter blasted the deck.

Anni slithered across the weather-bleached wood to the open door of the stairwell. Almost to the door, a gust caught her and she began sliding toward the edge. The helicopter roared overhead, trying to lift in the gale. Then a figure in a blue parka stepped out of the stairwell trailing a lifeline, got a grip on Anni and pulled her into the stairwell, out of the wind.

"Birgit!" Anni said. She was about to add her thanks, but Birgit turned away, to remove her safety harness and zip up her parka, but not before Anni saw she was carrying a gun. That had been the object pressing into Anni's side when Birgit had been manhandling her into the stairwell.

Birgit squinted at the helicopter; finally making it's way up into the low scud and disappearing to the West. She threw back the hood of her parka revealing a pretty, heart-shaped face with soft brown eyes, framed by long auburn hair. "You shouldn't have come out here."

Anni turned and started down the dank stairwell as Birgit unlatched the door, which slammed shut like the doors to hell closing.

"Phase has been out of synch for too long," Anni shouted back over her shoulder. "Karlstrom doesn't want to wait another three days while the storm clears."

She heard Birgit's steps clanking down behind her, so she hurried down to the door on the middle deck where the living space was.

Inside it was warm and light. The howling of the storm was muted.

Birgit caught up with her. Both women peeled off their parkas and threw them over the decrepit couch. Birgit stepped up to Anni, "Karlstrom said nothing to us."

"Your communications are lacking. No phones in this storm and the sea-bottom lines are unreliable."

Birgit stood in front of Anni, an inch taller, her slim body looking strong and fit in tight blue NSE coveralls. No sign of the gun.

Anni stepped around her. "I need to see Bengt immediately."

• • •

Gullveig Station was a steel cube, three stories high and sixty meters square, sitting twenty meters above the surface of the ocean on three gigantic concrete legs. Only the upper two decks were still habitable. Bengt and Birgit's living spaces, offices, the lounge and kitchen were all on the middle deck. The power monitoring equipment filled the top level, with the control room in the center. The lowest deck, still filled with abandoned oil piping gear was unmaintained and uninhabited. The bottom floor was so rusty in some areas it was unsafe to walk on.

• • •

Thirty years earlier, Gullveig had been an offshore oil platform called Shell BP XI. When North Sea oil had been depleted, Shell BP XI had been abandoned, being considered too expensive to move or demolish. Twenty years ago Nordstaatenergie, the Norwegian electrical power wholesaler headquartered in Stavanger Norway, refurbished it as a relay station for power beamed down from solar collectors in low earth orbit. From Gullveig, cables on the floor of the North Sea fed power to substations in Stavanger, Aberdeen, and Bremen. But now the geothermal plants were coming on line, with cheaper power, simpler extraction, new infrastructure. The smart money was moving out of orbital power and into geothermal.

NSE's management would have shut Gullveig Station down years ago except for the fact that they could not, by international law, abandon it. They would have to clean it, salvage what they could, and demolish the rest. Hundreds of millions of euros. But by chance, to reduce the genocidal bloodshed in Africa, the UN had voted a change in international law. This allowed warring tribes each to declare themselves a sovereign nation, a Free State. This was designed to reduce the endless racial bloodshed in central Africa. The tribes argued that current national boundaries were 'an outmoded and imperialistic remnant of colonial times' and should be abolished. Let the people define their own nations, their representatives argued persuasively in the UN General Assembly.

And so it was done.

Soon after, Nordstaatenergie, seeing a convenient way out of their ownership of the toxic asset that Gullveig had become, pushed through the necessary declaration to make Gullveig Station a Free State.

Company attorneys argued persuasively in the international court at the Hague, and since the station stood in international waters, and no one else was interested in it, the petition was quickly passed. Bengt Borreson, the lone inhabitant, and NSE's Station Manager, was given dual Norwegian and Gullveig citizenship and NSE removed two hundred million new euros of under-performing capital assets off their books. Gullveig Free State became a contractor selling power to Nordstaatenergie.

It hadn't taken Bengt Borreson long to realize certain new opportunities had become available to him. He had lived on the station for twenty years. His crew had been diminished year by year as the company automated much of the relay systems. And now Borreson lived alone. Which suited him fine, except for one thing. Not long after he became a Gullveig Free State citizen, he made a flight to Bucharest for a few days and spent his time in meetings with an employment firm. A few weeks later, a young Romanian woman had come through Oslo to Stavanger on a political refugee visa and presented herself at the Norge Avia office with a voucher signed by Borreson requesting transport to Gullveig.

Karlstrom, the Operations Manager, indignantly refused, but the NSE front office overruled him and told him to discreetly fly the woman to the station. They did not want her in Norway, where immigration authorities would soon be involved, and the whole legal fiction of Gullveig Free State would be reopened for public debate.

Bengt was told that as long as she remained invisible to NSE management, his "assistant" could stay on. The company kept no record of her in their files; the company had made it clear Bengt would pay her himself. The Norge Avia records of who was transported to the station were notoriously poor. Helicopter pilots wanted to fly, they didn't want to maintain accurate manifests. So Birgit Aaberg, as Bengt told people her name was, although she spoke no Norwegian, stayed on Gullveig. That had been two years ago. Everyone in Operations assumed that Birgit put up with Bengt in exchange for her Free State citizenship and her ticket out of Romania.

The station could actually operate untended except for monthly maintenance, but Borreson had convinced NSE's management to let him stay on until his retirement. Borreson argued that contingencies might emerge and he would be immediately present to deal with anything that might arise. Karlstrom knew Bengt was incompetent, so didn't want him in Operations in Stavanger, so there he stayed. "Let him stay out there, playing his games with this assistant," Karlstrom muttered, and left the issue alone.

The company chose to ignore all this as long as power flowed and there was no trouble on the station.

On Anni's monthly maintenance visits to the station, Birgit had seemed friendly. In the beginning almost fawningly so, and she was very deferential to Bengt. Anni assumed Birgit and Bengt had something more than a professional relationship. But as time went on, Birgit seemed wary of Anni and dismissive of Bengt. She had never been openly derisive of him for reasons that were obvious to all.

But Anni needed to talk to Bengt about his tampering with the phase management software, and her talking privately with Bengt was something Birgit would probably not like.

At deck two they went into a dank passageway, then through an ordinary wooden door and into the light and warmth of what resembled a down-at-the-heels office.

Birgit settled on the worn sofa, slipped on the tinted octagonal glasses she wore and regarded Anni.

"Operations in Stavanger said there would be no helicopter for four days, but you came." Birgit took out a brush and tried to untangle her hair.

Anni set her valise down, "Karlstrom is very unhappy." She had practiced the lie, and she said it convincingly. "The phase efficiency is two percentage points low and has been for a week now. Resetting the phase monitors can't wait any longer."

The last parts of what she said were true. Anni hoped the fact that she'd come out in the storm would add to the credibility of her story that the Operations Center was very unhappy about the continuing inefficiency, which meant lower profits.

Birgit glared at Anni over the tops of lavender lenses. "Karlstrom! Always he will blame us." She had switched from terrible Norwegian to bad English.

Anni put a sympathetic smile on her face. "Don't worry about him," Anni soothed. "I'll get to work on the adjustments right now."

"A few weeks, and then it will be bad again." Birgit snorted.

"That's why I fly out here every month."

Anni hoisted her valise, "I'll see you both in a few hours."

The subdued groaning of steel was all around them as the storm bent its back against Gullveig Station.

Anni went up an interior stair to the operations center. Here the megawatts of power being beamed down from orbit were received on floating mats, rectified to 350,000 volts, and fed into the seafloor cables that led to mainland Norway. The wall of red-lit gauges that monitored power dominated the room. The ceiling lighting was mostly inoperative, only a couple of tubes still working, but good enough to see what one was doing at any of the four workstations. Anni liked the old-style gauges because the heat they generated kept the room warmer than the rest of the station.

Anni sat down at a workstation, connected her computer, waited for the system data download, and started working.

She did not see Birgit open the door a crack and watch for a moment.

Three hours later, Anni had eighty percent of

the phase synchronizers reset; power was within one percent of maximum efficiency. She stood up, stretched, then sat down again and ran a general check of the operating systems.

• • •

Time for a drink or two. Her expression hardened. And time to ingratiate herself with Bengt.

She stood in the red glow of the wall dials, thinking.

Sex with him would be distasteful, but no worse than with some of the other men she'd had to manipulate to get to where she was. Moreover, she might be able to use that as blackmail to keep him from talking about this scheme to Birgit.

Anni went down one level to the living quarters where Bengt had made himself comfortable in the suite of offices, cafeteria, recreation, and sleeping rooms built for the oil platform's crew of thirty. Plenty of room.

In her past visits, Anni had explored some of the empty rooms, but the dank bareness of painted steel walls, the scent of saltwater, the gloom, had depressed her and she retreated back to the suite of six rooms that Bengt had converted to his "Little Kingdom in the Sea," as he called it.

She opened the large bulkhead door and went down a birchwood-paneled corridor and through an opened glass door. There was shag carpet on the floor here, dirty, but better than bare steel.

• • •

When Anni entered his office, Bengt rose unsteadily, and leaned on his littered desk. He was a short, pleasant looking Norwegian, dressed in gray slacks and military-cut white shirt with the sleeves rolled up. He had been handsome once. Now his blond hair had thinned, his belly gone to fat, and both his complexion and his bloodshot pale blue eyes were dulled by drink and lack of natural sunlight.

He topped up his glass from a bottle of akvavit and poured a glass for Anni.

"So nice to see you, Annifrida," he enunciated carefully in English. He lumbered around the desk, drinks in hand, and threw himself heavily down on one Scandia chair. Anni accepted her glass then carefully seated herself on the sofa opposite the table from Bengt. He sat, listlessly staring at Anni's chest.

Anni sipped at her drink and blinked rapidly. "You don't have wine, do you?"

Bengt brightened and lurched to his feet. "Yes, wine. I have. A special treat. I had the pilot bring it last month."

He rummaged in a cabinet and extracted a bottle of wine, then more rummaging for an opener.

"I've completed most of the phase monitor adjustments," Anni said. "That should make Karlstrom happy for a while. But you let the efficiency stay low for over a week…"

"The storm…"

"This was before the storm," Anni said as if she was correcting a child who'd been caught lying.

Bengt slopped wine into a glass and handed it to her then seated himself beside her on the sofa.

The wine was a cheap Australian Syrah from the duty free shop at Stavanger Airport.

"I love your Japanese eyes, Annifrida, so…" words eluded him.

"If you keep letting phase monitors stay out of synch, you may be asked to retire early," Anni said, trying to lead the conversation to manual manipulation of phase monitoring. But Bengt did not take the hint.

He raised his glass in a toast.

"Karlstrom. The high and mighty Chief of Operations. He thinks he is king, but he would have nothing without this station, and me. And Birgit,"

Bengt downed his drink and set his glass on the stained Birchwood coffee table with exaggerated care.

"I know you have been meddling with the phase monitors, Bengt," Anni said directly, but in what she hoped was a neutral tone.

Bengt stared at the cheerful fire glowing in the video screen's faux fireplace. He seemed not to hear her.

The room shuddered slightly as a slow resonance crept up the concrete legs of the station.

Bengt jerked his glass to his lips, found it was empty, and refilled it from the Akvavit bottle.

"I know you manually reset the phase monitors twice in the last two weeks," Anni repeated, tired of being subtle.

"I don't know what you are talking about."

His breath was thick with alcohol.

"If I report you to Karlstrom, you'll be fired, not retired." *But then Karlstrom would know about my software changes,* Anni thought. *I've got to get this oaf to admit he's doing it, and then agree to leaving any manipulation to me for a cut of the profits.*

Bengt grinned, "Annifrida. I do not adjust the phase... I leave that to you." He slid his arm along the back of the sofa and around her.

She kept herself from pulling away at first, but she did pull away when he tried to kiss her.

"You look tired," she said softly with a seducer's voice. His face was sagging toward sleep. "Let's go take a nap," she said. She took his hand and led him into the bedroom and sat him down on the bed. Anni suffered through some clumsy pawing while she removed his shoes and helped him stretch out on the stained, evil-smelling bed.

She left him snoring and returned to the living room. She thought she heard the soft sigh of the glass doors at the end of the corridor, but it was impossible to tell with the noise of the storm all around.

She stood thinking. *Nothing more I can do until he sobers up.*

She went up to the control room and logged in to the power management system and sat for a moment watching the red lines running left to right, endlessly changing, like medical monitors attached to some gigantic living creature, rows of lines flickering in spikes and valleys, flowing across the screen. The flow of power, the flow of money. It was hypnotic. Gullveig's output was now running efficiently. The adjustments she'd made would keep efficiency up for a few weeks, then the ancient analog monitors would drift out of alignment again. But so what, it was job security for her.

Unless that fool Borreson keeps doing something so stupid even Karlstrom can't ignore.

• • •

A deck below, Bengt snored peacefully in his bed. The booming wind didn't disturb his drunken slumber, but the click of the door latch did.

"Anni?" he slurred, sitting up. There was no light on in the room. A slim form stepped out of the dim light of the opened doorway.

"Anni, you…"

Birgit put the muzzle of her Mauser 10 mm pistol against his chest and fired twice. Bengt's body snapped back onto the bed. He gurgled up blood, his mouth opened in a silent scream. She put the gun to his head and fired once more. His body convulsed sickeningly, then he lay still. The great girders below them creaked as the North Sea was driven to greater fury by the Arctic wind. Birgit, with some difficulty, managed to get Bengt's beefy form wrapped in a blanket so she could drag it out of the bedroom, down the corridor, and out into the steel-walled exterior of the station.

• • •

She pried the latches open on an emergency hatch and the freezing wind sucked down from holes and open hatches above nearly pulled her out. But the wind made it easier to wrestle Bengt's still-warm body up to the lip of the hatch and shove it out into the night. She left the hatch open and went back for the remaining bedding and hurled it out into the storm.

As she did so, she noted that her flesh felt wet. Glancing down at her NSE uniform, she saw that it was not sweat but blood and gore that had soaked through her clothing, dripping down onto her boots. Quickly she stripped off her clothing and shoes, and rolled them into a ball. She stood naked; her lithe form lashed by the chill, wet winds, and fed the clothes to the hatch. She laughed, not feeling the cold, as the torrent of mist cleansed her skin.

After stopping by her room to pick up a fresh uniform, Birgit retreated to the warmth of the stateroom and poured herself a generous portion of akvavit and sat down at Bengt's desk. On the auxiliary control console she activated the communication link and typed: "Emergency notification! General manager Bengt Borreson was blown overboard and lost at sea at 2230 hours today while attempting to secure an inductor relay terminal. I am maintaining normal operations."

Birgit stared at the message for a moment, then typed "Birgit Aaberg, acting station manager," and put the message in the outgoing box. The system was fully functional, but very slow. The company had a communications link to Operations in Stavanger run through one of the old oil distribution pipelines, but it was text only, no voice, no video. And it took its time. One typed a message, put it in the outbound message box, and waited for the automated system to fit it in with the gigabytes of data flowing from Gullveig to the Operations Center. It might be an hour until it reached Operations.

Birgit sipped the fiery Akvavit, then deleted that message and, typing slowly and carefully, wrote a new one.

"Bengt Borreson and Annifrida Hellstrom were both blown overboard..."

She put the message in the outgoing box and logged off.

Then she ejected the magazine from her Mauser. Five rounds left, more than enough. She snapped it back into the gun and started up the dark stairwell toward the control room.

• • •

In the control room, Anni opened another screen on her laptop, and bypassed Bengt's crude security, an off-the-shelf Alpha Codex two years out of date, made a note of his passwords, and found there were two messages waiting to go out. She opened the newest one.

It was addressed to Karlstrom in Operations. After the usual apologies for low efficiency it went on to say, "...regret to inform you I believe Ms. Annifrida Hellstrom is tampering with the phase management system…"

"That bastard," she whispered. "Blaming me for the low efficiency. And apparently he knows about my software despite his lying to me just now."

Anni deleted that message and opened the second one. Although it was from Bengt's password protected address it was actually from Birgit to the Bank of Gullveig at the Neu Bank, Luxembourg, asking for confirmation of a recent ten thousand new euro deposit.

"That bitch," Anni murmured. She leaned back in the decrepit chair. "She's the one manually overriding the phase management software and playing the Geneva spot power market."

Anni made note of the bank account number, and stared at the message. *Birgit. I need to find her fast and get her on my side. Forget about Borreson.*

The steady whistle of wind coming through the multiple holes and leaking hatches in the station, changed pitch. Anni raised her head and listened but it did not change again. Steel groaned and creaked and the ocean was a subdued roar behind the reassuring hum of the ancient electronics.

There was no time to lose.

A new message appeared in the outbox but she didn't take time to read it. She pulled on her sweater and started for the door, which opened as she approached, revealing Birgit with a pistol in her hand aimed at Anni.

Anni dived behind the control console and crawled as fast as she could down the length of it toward the door on the other side of the room. The dim light and the noise of the storm and the old electronics might give her some cover.

Halfway, she reversed course and scrambled back toward the door Birgit had come in. Anni peeked around the console. Sure enough, Birgit had assumed Anni would try for the other door and was rounding the opposite end of the long console.

Instantly, Anni was on her feet, and in three long strides she was out the door. The steel doorframe flashed passed her as she flung herself down the stairs, taking the steps four at a time.

She sped all the way down to deck one, then into the dark maze of abandoned rooms.

In the darkness, Anni paused gasping for breath. She heard footsteps on the stairs. She turned and made her way into the next room and the next, dodging jumbled equipment as best she could in what lighting there was that still worked. The floor was crunchy with rust; the emergency lights were on in some rooms, others were pitch black. She ran into something big which knocked her down. Some piece of abandoned oil-rig gear unidentifiable in the darkness. Carefully she stood and slowed down, moving as quietly as possible, trying to think where Birgit would go—and where she should go.

Slowing down, Anni made her way carefully through rooms ghostly with shrouded machinery. The noise of the storm was much louder on this deck.

She knew that below the steel plates she walked on there was nothing except the heaving waves of the icy North Sea. Fall through, and it would be certain death.

She moved cautiously, silently, listening for any sound from Birgit amidst the roar of wind and waves.

• • •

Anni knew there were three stairwells leading up, two enclosed the exterior stairwells and one set of stairs in the middle. She'd try for the middle one. She moved forward trying to walk near the bulkheads where the steel was less rusty.

She moved from dark room to dark room. She realized cold air was blowing past her now. Probably roaring down through the center stairwell, the storm wind creating a reverse chimney effect, pulling air out the bottom of the station.

As she crept along, she saw open hatches and rusted-through holes leading down to Aegir's deeps. If she slipped into any of the openings, she'd be pulled down in an instant.

She stepped as carefully as she could, her heart freezing when a bubble of rust gave way, but so far the floor plates under her feet had held.

The roaring chimney was close, maybe two more rooms.

Two more rooms and she was there, the stairwell up. It was in a large room and in the floor was a hatch, over it a chain hoist. The oilmen had used it to bring equipment into the station from ships below.

The hatch top lay open on its hinges, a howling tornado blew fiercely down through the opening. Occasionally there was the glitter of light reflected off the mountainous waves passing below.

As Anni skirted the open hatch and stepped quickly toward the stairs, Birgit emerged from the shadows behind the stairwell leveling the gun at her.

Without breaking stride, Anni lowered her head and dove at Birgit's feet. The gun roared but the bullet missed Anni. Anni got inside Birgit's gun arm and the two women tumbled among the equipment thrashing and slugging each other. The gun went off again, deafening Anni, but this time she got a good grip on Birgit's gun hand and slammed it against the bulkhead. The gun skittered away into the shadows, but Birgit twisted free from Anni's grip and punched Anni hard in the body and in the face. Anni danced back over a coil of steel cable and came within centimeters of the open hatch and its murderous downdraft. Birgit, her face twisted with rage, leapt at Anni. Anni held onto the cable and kicked at Birgit, pushing her flying body sideways. Birgit hit the deck, rolled into the hatch coaming and the downdraft pulled her down through the hatch into the roaring darkness of wind and waves below.

But she had not fallen to her death in the North Sea. Anni saw Birgit's elegant fingers gripping the edge of the hatch as she dangled, unable to pull herself up against the downdraft.

Anni kicked over the heavy hatch cover and the wind slammed it shut like a trap.

In the dim light, severed fingers rolled away from the steel hatch cover.

Forcing back a gag, Anni jumped to her feet and ran up two flights of stairs to the red-lit control room. She closed the door and stood gasping for air. After a moment, she sat down at a workstation and let the red glow and warmth soothe her until her shaking subsided. After a moment she noticed there was a message waiting to go out. A message signed by Birgit.

Anni read it, her eyebrows climbing "Bengt lost overboard? Anni lost overboard? Birgit acting manager?"

Anni checked that the antiquated messaging system had not yet sent the message out, and then put it on hold. She hurried down one deck to Bengt's suite. No one there, and the bed had been stripped of sheets and blankets. She searched the entire deck, but Bengt was gone.

Anni snagged the half empty bottle of wine off Bengt's coffee table and returned to the control room where she sat staring at Birgit's message, swigging from the wine bottle.

"You killed Bengt, didn't you, Birgit? Threw him overboard when he was passed out. And you tried to kill me. Might have succeeded if I hadn't noticed you were carrying a gun. Probably planning to shoot me as soon as the helicopter was out of sight. And it was you, not Bengt, who was scamming the company… like I am. Going to build yourself a nice cash reserve, then emigrate to Germany, maybe as a Free State citizen." Anni slugged down more wine.

Anni deleted Birgit's still unsent message.

She logged in as Bengt, and certified herself Gullveig Free State citizenship, back-dating it to when she first arrived at the station and put it in the out-going message buffer.

Then she logged in as herself and wrote a second message: "Station manager Bengt Borreson and assistant Birgit Aaberg lost overboard at 0100 while attempting to repair an auxiliary relay in the storm."

She signed it "Annifrida Hellstrom, acting station manager." After a minute she went back and deleted the word "acting."

She staggered to her feet, exhausted, and stumbled down the stairs and into an empty bunkroom far from Bengt's suite. She pulled her parka around her, "Next visit, I'm bringing some decent wine." The boom of the storm seemed to be diminishing.

• • •

The next morning in the Nordstaatenergie operations center in Stavanger, a young operator called Karlstrom over and showed him the two messages from Gullveig.

"Two deaths," Karlstrom mused. "No evidence, I'm sure. No witnesses except Annifrida." He grinned at the younger man seated in front of the screen. "An old facility in the middle of the North Sea… many dangers… there have been accidents in the past." He spread his hands. "I will notify Security and they will get a statement from Ms. Hellstrom when she returns to Stavanger. In the meantime, the power flows, the phase efficiency is good. Anni has solved our problem."

Tanker at Risk

Pirates hijack an oil tanker, threatening to blow up the ship if a ransom is not paid. Jason is hired to pay them off. Face to face with the pirates, he finds himself bargaining for his life as well as millions of dollars of crude oil.

Jason Wolfe had flown helicopters long enough to know that the Somali pirate flying the ancient Huey out to the tanker was barely competent to keep the helicopter straight and level. But he said nothing. The other pirate's pistol pressed to the back of his head was clear enough warning. Jason clutched the briefcase with two million dollars in it and kept his attention on the lights of the ship below.

Finally, the helicopter wobbled down to a bounce-and-skid landing on the tanker's vast foredeck, and

Jason was forced out of the Huey into a humid sea breeze overlaid with the smell of crude oil.

Two Somalis waited for him. One aimed a pistol at him while the other relieved him of the briefcase. They motioned for him to follow them across the expanse of deck to the superstructure and up four flights of steel steps to the bridge. In a roomy cabin, the man who'd taken the briefcase from him opened it and examined the money. The man with the gun waved Jason into the next cabin and, in East European-accented English, said, "Sit here."

Jason sat down at the spacious conference table. Two video cameras on tripods were aimed at Jason with their red lights on. Jason's briefcase was on the table beside a speaker phone.

Two Somalis with AK-47s marched Captain Iannota into the room and sat him at the table beside Jason. Incongruously, the steward brought a pot of tea and several white cups bearing the crest of the ship they were on, the *Epic Circle*. The Somalis poured their tea and drank it. The East European was not offered any.

Another Somali entered the room carrying Jason's new Iridium phone. He handed it to Jason. "Connect your phone to this speaker and contact Mr. Headley."

Jason did so and Headley answered on the first ring.

The Somali stepped into camera range and read from a script: "You will arrange the release of twelve Somali nationals currently being illegally held by the American government in a CIA detention facility in Ethiopia. The press will be given a statement from your government retracting the false piracy charges against them. The names are being transmitted to your phone now. If these demands are not met in two hours, we will kill your messenger. If these demands are not met in four hours, we will kill the captain. If they are not met in six hours we will scuttle this ship."

He terminated the call and two gunmen marched Jason and Iannota down two decks and locked them in a cabin. There was nothing in the cabin except a steel bunk, a toilet and a porthole too small to wriggle through.

Iannota sat down on the bunk and stared at the wall.

• • •

The terrace of the Marina Restaurant was uncrowded on a weekday morning. "I can't believe you went back to work for Headley," Marisa scolded Jason. "Six months ago, when you quit, you told me you hated the guy." The water sparkled in the L.A. sun. Yellow and blue sailboats with gleaming chrome fittings bobbed gently at their moorings. Marisa had lived in Marina Del Rey for six years now. Ever since she and Jason had both quit working for Gary Headley and Fidelity Investments.

"We sat right here in this restaurant," Marisa said. "And you told me in no uncertain terms that you'd never work for the guy again. You were going to Hawaii. Use your helicopter license to fly tourists. You were through with eighty hour work weeks and sleazy stock deals."

"I spent ten months flying sightseers around Maui in a purple helicopter making minimum wage." Jason grinned tightly. "No benefits of course, just hourly wage. And, oh yeah, I was supposed to sweep up the office and make coffee when I wasn't flying. No thanks. I need more challenge—more future—than that."

Marisa eyed him, "Sounds better than working for Headley."

Jason squinted into the glitter on the water. "I need the money. Unlike me, you did pretty well."

"Saved my money," Marisa said. "Kept my license, do my own small scale trading, make a comfortable living. And best of all no Headley and that pack of sharks he deals with."

She gave him a look over the top of her sunglasses. "You're too nice a guy to be working for Headley."

"News calls him a patriot. Trying to maintain America's energy supply."

"Manipulate it, you mean," Marisa retorted.

Jason shook his head. "I'm flying out to Singapore tomorrow. An emergency…"

"Everything's an emergency with him." She shook her head. "I'd be very careful if I were you. He will sacrifice you like a used tissue."

"The money's good…"

"Not if you're dead," she said.

• • •

Fidelity Corporation's Gulfstream 550 slanted down through the night toward Singapore's Changi Airport. Jason was the only passenger on the long flight from Los Angeles to Honolulu, a fuel stop at Guam, then Singapore.

Elwin Chen, Fidelity's agent with FirstAsia Bank, was at the Exec terminal to meet him. "Headley wants to talk to you right now."

Jason pulled out his phone but Elwin shook his head. "No. Over the secure line at the bank."

They rode the limo through clean streets to

FirstAsia's glass tower. Outside the floor-to-ceiling windows on the penthouse level, the lights of Singapore lay in neat lines. The lights of the oil refineries glittered like jewels.

"Headley directed us to cash $2 million US out of our arbitrage account," Chen's normally cheerful face was pressed into a frown. "He said it was an emergency."

"Everything's an emergency with him," Jason said.

"We're already overextended, the US dollar is way down against other currencies, and I'm supposed to debit two million dollars and hand it to you in cash? This is crazy."

Jason said nothing as they marched down the hall to an interior, secure, conference room.

The video link was already on. On screen was Headley's private office bathed in pale Los Angeles light. Jason sat down and Elwin Chen pressed the 'activate' button. In a moment Gary Headley seated himself in front of the camera. He was dressed in a charcoal-colored Armani suit and red Brioni tie. Over his dour face, his graying hair was combed straight back.

"We've got a situation, Jason" Headley said. "The *Epic Circle*, a 520,000-barrel VLCC. She's in the Straits, enroute back to the Gulf."

"These pirates hijacked an empty tanker?" Jason said.

Headley nodded.

"I assume you've got Triple Canopy working this," Jason said.

"Not this time. I need you to work it alone."

Jason took a deep breath. "Better to have backup. Too easy for them to kill me, disappear with the ransom money."

Headley pushed a button on the desk. "Here's the video we got this morning." A picture-in-picture came on the screen showing a sad-looking Greek man looking at papers on a table in front of him. Two masked gunmen stood behind him. Someone off-camera prompted him and he looked up and said, "I am Arkis Iannota, captain of the *Epic Circle*," then he read from a script that demanded two million dollars and the release of twelve Somali prisoners being held by the CIA.

When he was done, the picture-in-picture disappeared and Headley leaned toward the camera. "Get two million in cash in front of them ASAP, Jason. The State Department has already assured me they'll release the Somali prisoners," Headley made a dismissive motion. "They're small fry. Not important. They're being flown to Beirut right now to make sure the media covers the event. You need to get cash in front of these hijackers within," Headley checked his watch, "three hours. Then they can take the money and disappear, and this thing is resolved before they decide to start killing people and playing politics on YouTube."

"Only two million?" Jason asked. "They don't know what a tanker is worth?"

Headley ignored the question and said, "Elwin has the money for you, Jason. Get it to the pirates fast." Headley turned contemplative. "Who formed Christ, but Herod and Caesar?" Headley quoted. "Violence, the bloody sire of the world's values." He unfolded his long frame out of his chair. "Get this fixed fast, Jason. Before they start shooting people."

The screen went dark.

"The money's in this briefcase," Chen said handing Jason a new, leather briefcase. "Was that quote from the Bible?" Chen asked.

Jason said opened the briefcase and quickly ascertained the money was there. He snapped it shut. "It's a quote from the poet Robinson Jeffers. He used to give us a quote every week at the staff meeting." *Pompous jerk*, Jason added mentally.

Elwin Chen drove Jason to an executive airfield at the back of Changi Airport. "The Singapore police let the pirates land a helicopter here. It'll take you to the ship." The limo stopped at a row of expensive commercial helicopters. Down at the end Jason saw an ancient military helicopter, its insignia and numbers painted over. "Want me to call somebody for you?" Chen said. "You need some kind of backup."

"No time," Jason said. He stepped out into the humid night and walked down the silent row of helicopters.

The cargo door slid open and a Somali stepped out. Even in the heat he kept his Adidas jacket zipped up, there was a conspicuous bulge of a holstered weapon. There were shadows of others in the cargo space. "In front," he said in English.

Jason scrambled into the right front seat as the turbine started to spool up. He felt the barrel of a pistol press against his neck. The Somali pilot lifted off with a scrape and jolt.

• • •

In the locked cabin of the tanker, Iannota began to speak in a monotone. "It makes little difference if your boss is successful in arranging the prisoner release. These men will kill us anyway."

"Makes no sense," Jason said. "If they kill us, they'll have government troops as well as oil company mercenaries after them. They're better off taking the money and disappearing. These things have happened before."

"This is different. The hijackers need to kill us to give them credibility in the world media when they unveil their trump card."

"What are you talking about?"

"The operations center of International Transport, the company that operates this ship for Fidelity Investments, has GPS monitors and telemetry sensors on this ship and all their ships. Right now it shows we are on course at marker 1140 in the Malacca Straits. IT's cargo monitoring telemetry shows that the ship is empty of oil, which is correct. But telemetry shows tank status green, which is not correct, since they have rewired the sensors. The tanks are full of explosive oil fumes." Iannota looked grim. "If a spark were to ignite those fumes, the tanks would explode and this ship would sink."

"That makes even less sense," Jason said. "This ship is worth a lot more than the two million they asked for."

Iannota continued to stare at the wall. "The cash

and prisoner release are diversions. The terrorists are playing for higher stakes. The Malacca Straits are quite shallow here. If this ship is sunk in the channel, the wreckage will block the channel. All the crude oil that comes from the Middle East to Asia comes through this channel. The refineries will run out of crude oil in about two weeks."

Jason gave him a hard look, "And as soon as news gets out that the Straits are blocked, fuel prices all over Asia will skyrocket. There will be an inflationary spike like the one in 1997 that wiped out Thailand's economy and put Japan into recession." Jason leaned forward. "China will dump the billions of US dollars she's been hoarding onto the world market and that will push the debt-ridden US economy into recession."

Jason and Iannota heard the door lock turn. The East European came into the room with two Somalis behind him. Jason and Iannota were marched back to the table in front of the video cameras. Jason was pushed down into the chair. Iannota was told to stand to one side. The video cameras were running. The European stepped forward, his pistol held in both hands. He aimed it at Jason's face.

There was a faraway burst of automatic weapons fire. The European turned the Somalis jumped to the windows, and Jason whirled, grabbed the gun, and he and the European went over the chair, struggling for the pistol. It went off once and a ricochet spanged around the steel walls. They hit the deck hard and rolled against one leg of the table, which was bolted to the deck, giving Jason enough leverage to wrench the European's forearm up and back. He heard the elbow joint crackle as tendons tore loose, and then Jason had the gun. He sprang up, kicked the European in the face, and crouched to face the Somalis.

But they were gone.

There was automatic weapon fire on the deck below. Jason edged out the open door. A group of camouflage-clad men were exchanging fire with scattered hijackers. Men crouched behind deck-fittings, firing in all directions. Several dead hijackers lay crumpled on the deck.

Headley must have called in Triple Canopy's mercenaries after all, Jason thought as he ran down the stairs. *I'll lay low until the fighting stops and I can surrender to them.*

A man stepped into the corridor ahead of Jason, raised his machine pistol. There was a burst from the deck below and the man staggered, his weapon clattering to the deck. Jason scooped up the MAC11 he'd dropped and ducked into the stairwell, hiding in the shadow.

Iannota came down the stairs fast.

Jason grabbed his arm. "We stay out of sight until the mercenaries have overpowered the hijackers and defused the bombs, then we can..." Jason started.

Iannota shifted the briefcase to his left hand, pulled out a pistol and aimed it at Jason.

"Into the helicopter," Iannota commanded.

Jason stared, then comprehension dawned. They went down the back corridor and out into the night. The helipad was behind the superstructure, away from the fighting on the foredeck.

Iannota followed Jason into the ancient Huey. "Take off," Iannota shouted.

"If we take off, the mercenaries will try to shoot us down," Jason said.

"Go."

Jason clicked the switches on, engaged the turbine starter and let it wind up to start-power. Then he engaged the turbine, hit the fuel injectors, watched the RPM come up. He engaged the tail rotor. A round banged through the aluminum hull of the helicopter. Thirty more seconds to minimum RPM. Jason forced himself to sit watching the rotor RPM slowly increasing. More shots were fired, two hit the aluminum skin of the helicopter.

The turbine reached minimum RPM and Jason jammed the blade-angle full-on, eased the collective up and the ancient craft shuddered into the air, scrapped a skid across a handrail, then dipped down toward the dark ocean. Jason let it drop until he felt surface effect off the ocean, then pitched the helicopter forward praying the old turbines would take full emergency power. The dark cliff of the tanker's hull receded behind them.

Jason's hands were shaking so severely the helicopter wobbled. He loosened his grip on the stick and the collective and focused his mind on flying.

"Turn to heading 190," Iannota shouted above the din.

There were empty holes in the aluminum dashboard where instruments had been cannibalized, but the ancient magnetic compass was still there. Jason banked carefully to heading 190, throttled back to cruise speed, and brought the aircraft to straight and level flight at 1500 feet.

The deserted coast of Sumatra was a wall of black jungle in the moonlight. Iannota instructed him to fly parallel to the shore. There were no lights; the jungle was entirely unmarked by human habitation. Then a makeshift jetty with generator-powered lights came into view. There were some ramshackle buildings behind the jetty and a single outdoor light showing a dirt road stretching away into the jungle.

"Follow the road," Iannota ordered.

After a few moments, a deserted building appeared at a wide spot in the road. Jason saw a car parked by the building.

"Land in the road."

Jason brought the helicopter down in a whirl of dust.

"Get out," Iannota said brusquely. The spool-down of the turbine was loud in the jungle silence.

Iannota marched Jason to the car. Behind him he heard Iannota open the car door, toss the briefcase in, then close it again. The night was still and the air carried the moldy smell of dry-season jungle. Jason turned and saw Iannota now had Jason's black Iridium phone in his left hand.

"Go to the wall," Iannota said. Broken glass crunched as Jason stepped slowly toward the wall.

"You were in on this from the start, weren't you?" Jason said. "You helped the hijackers get aboard and set the bombs. Now you're going to take the two million, blow the tanker, and disappear."

"After I complete one last task," Iannota said, pushing buttons on the phone.

Dread bloomed in Jason's mind. "You actually are going to sink the ship aren't you? You'll set off the bombs by remote control from my phone."

"Your boss's idea." Iannota said. He'd finished dialing. "Then I'm going to kill you."

• • •

Night in downtown Los Angeles, the Santa Ana winds had blown the smog out to sea and the stars glittered as brightly as the lights of the skyscrapers and the rivers of freeway traffic.

Gary Headley stood at the window of his private suite facing the Hollywood Hills. The ghostly image of his face lay superimposed on the lights of the Hollywood Hills. He was holding one of the customized black Iridium phones.

He crossed to the row of screens at one side of his desk and studied the numbers flickering there. Then he went back to the window overlooking the nightscape, entered an encryption and a number on the black phone, paused for a second, then pressed "send." There was a thin squeal from the phone, then nothing. He switched it off, wrapped it in the

L.A. Times and went down to his Mercedes in the parking garage. He selected a Mahler symphony from the satellite radio feed and drove down Interstate 10 freeway toward his spacious home in Pacific Palisades. At a freeway exit chosen at random, he pulled into a gas station and tossed the newspaper and phone into a trash can.

• • •

"Wait," Jason told Iannota. The deserted building smelled of old urine. Something skittered near his feet—a lizard or a cockroach. He took a deep breath, preparing to dive at Iannota even though he was three meters away. He had to try, or in less than a minute he would be dead.

Jason saw Ianotta standing, phone to his ear, the gun aimed at Jason.

Jason sprang, the gun went off with a roar, and then a second explosion slammed Jason down onto the cracked asphalt. He rolled to his feet and staggered toward Iannota, but the captain lay on the ground. The left side of his head blown away. Blood pooled, black as oil in the moonlight.

Jason was shaking so hard he could barely stand. "A bomb in my phone." The jungle's night noises resumed. He stared down at Iannota's body. "This is not what I want, none of this." He got the car keys out of Iannota's pocket and drove away.

• • •

The Santa Ana winds had blown themselves out, and Los Angeles lay still and warm under a hazy sky. The waters of Marina Del Rey glittered in late afternoon sun. Jason strolled into Marina restaurant and crossed to Marisa at a table under a blue and yellow umbrella. She hugged him.

"I would say you look smug," Jason said, taking a chair. "But I don't want to sound curmudgeonly."

Marisa laughed her big laugh. "You look a little ragged around the edges."

He forced a grin. "Go ahead and say 'I told you so.' " Two glasses of a Paso Robles Cabernet Sauvignon appeared. They toasted. "I'm finished with Headley," Jason sighed. "Permanently."

Marisa nodded, "I hope you mean it this time."

He told her the whole story.

"Well, Headley's smart," Marisa said. "He managed to bump oil spot market prices up for a few hours, took his profits, covered Fidelity's over-extension, then used Triple Canopy to capture his own tanker back. Asia's oil supply is once again secure, and he ends up the media hero of the day."

Jason squinted at the sun-sparkle on the water.

"Hero of the day," Jason repeated softly. "Convincing the media that the tanker captain went rogue and conspired with the hijackers to take the tanker, get cash, blackmail some Somali pirates out of jail..."

"By the way," Marisa interrupted. "What happened to the ransom money?"

Jason, embarrassed, studied his wine glass. "I returned it to Elwin Chen."

"I knew you would. You're honest. That's why you should stay away from Headley and those sharks on the exchange."

"Murdering sharks," Jason said carefully. "It's one thing to kill each other's portfolio on the stock exchange. But killing people in real life...Headley murdered Iannota."

She nodded. "And he'll get away with it." Marisa studied Jason. "That phone-bomb was meant for you, Jason. You know that."

He gazed into his wine glass, frowning.

"Headley planned to kill you," Marisa continued. "You knew too much, the financial situation at Fidelity, Iannota, the effect of a scuttled tanker in the straits. You could put two and two together."

"I should expose him in court."

"Don't bother. It's yesterday's news. The crisis is over, Triple Canopy's mercenaries brought the pirates into custody..."

"Killing a few in the process.."

"So Headley can say Iannota was killed in the fighting." She took his hand and squeezed it hard. "You have no proof anything. Think you'd want to argue the case? If so, where? Malaysian court?" The tanker was Greek flagged. The Straits are considered international."

Jason slid his chair back a little and crossed his legs, luxuriating in the sun. "For all my effort, I didn't even get paid. I'm out of a job and flat broke." He gave her a wan smile.

"You're not going back to Headley," Marisa said flatly. "I won't let you."

They sat quietly, admiring the water and the sailboats at their slips.

Marisa said, "In the news Headley is spouting all his usual Robinson Jeffers quotes. The newsies probably think Headley wrote that stuff himself. They've been using it to describe Headley," Marisa struck a noble pose. "He belongs to stormy skies and heavy seas."

"What a bunch of bull," Jason said.

Marisa rummaged in her purse. "Maybe this will help you decide on a new career." She handed him a plain white envelope. Inside was a cashier's check from Marisa's stock trading LLC for $260,000. It was made out to him.

"The other night," Marisa said meditatively, "As I was watching all this play out in the oil spot market price on the London exchange, I couldn't resist doing a little speculation for the both of us. We made a few dollars. That's your half."

"Really? Thanks."

"Well," she said with a mischievous smile. "Like Headley, maybe you and I also belong to stormy skies."

They raised their glasses in a toast. "Slightly cloudy skies maybe," Jason said. "Not stormy."

Blood

Matt discovers his supervisor, the team leader of a biochemical weapons research team, has been murdered. But before Matt can notify the police, he is kidnapped by the agency's section chief, who may himself be the killer.

The November wind whistled down K Street, but Matt was sweating as he approached the unmarked door to his design lab. No sign identified the faceless limestone building.

The lock released on the second swipe of his key card. *Hell of a note when the National Institute of Health needs security locks and guards.* Inside, he held up his picture ID up to the security guards, passed through the metal detector, and walked down the corridor to his office.

At his desk with the two big screens, Matt connected

the external drive he was carrying with him, and displayed the mem rotor design he had revised. He and Nakamishi had worked on the mem design for two long years. Robyn had begun to jokingly accuse him of seeing another woman on the nights he came home at eleven o'clock. However, he could see her growing disappointment as they spent less and less time together. It bothered him, but his work was important.

Last week she'd gone home, to Montreal, to visit her family. Matt missed her badly.

He forced his mind back to the micro electronic machine—the mem—displayed on his screen. Matt had done the rotor design, Nakamishi everything else. Their design consisted of a microscopic disk the size of a blood hemoglobin platelet, inside which was a tiny rotor and a ring of hexagonal storage cells. The mem's casing was a chitin-like synthetic with slots around the rim. A silicon wafer, masked during the casting process, was later etched to form a free-turning rotor over the ring of hexagonal storage cells. The micro-milliamp currents continuously coursing through nerve synapses in the human body provided power to turn the rotor. When activated, the turning rotor broke the seals over the slots in the wafer rim and pumped the fluid held in the storage cells into the bloodstream.

The mems were microscopic. A hundred thousand of them could be invisibly suspended in a 10 CC saline solution and injected into a vein.

"A breakthrough in drug delivery," Sinqueford's memo had trumpeted a week ago, when he'd received the draft results of Nakamishi's design effort. Matt was proud Nakamishi had listed him as co-principal investigator, even though Matt was a brand-new PhD, and had done perhaps ten percent of the work. Nakamishi was a generous, unambitious man.

Matt checked his rotor etchant revision once more, then searched for the design file, where he could upload his revision. But after ten frustrating moments he could find nothing, no design file, none of Nakamishi's preliminary designs, no backup files. Nothing.

But hidden away behind the Dalek-Exterminate password he and Nakamishi had jokingly set up, he found a cryptic message, dated the previous day at noon.

"Avoid Sinqueford. Destroy design files."

Matt stared at his screen. This made no sense. *This is the National Institute of Health, for God's sake. Not the Defense Department.*

Mary, the section chief's secretary, popped her head into Matt's office. "Mr. Sinqueford has been waiting for you since eight o'clock this morning," she snapped. "Get up to his office now!"

Matt glanced at the clock. Nine-fifteen. "Sorry . . ."

"Read your email," Mary snapped. She slammed the door.

Matt spent a few more frustrating moments searching for the mem design file on their usual server, on the cloud, everywhere he could think of, but there was no longer a file by that name anywhere. He pawed through Nakamishi's desk drawer for the external drive he knew Nakamishi kept there. It, too, was gone. Matt went back to his computer and stared at the screen. "Avoid Sinqueford . . ."

His phone buzzed. A text from Mary demanded "GET UP HERE NOW!" Matt ejected his external drive from his computer and put it in his pocket. Nakamishi or someone else had deleted the main and backup design files; the only remaining full copy was the one on the external drive Matt had taken home last night.

Matt deleted Nakamishi's warning, slipped his coat back on, and left the building.

Outside, it had gotten windy. Matt walked briskly

down the block and turned left on Pennsylvania Avenue, thinking furiously. Recently Nakamishi had seemed uncharacteristically distracted and furtive. Matt had dismissed it as pressure from Sinqueford, who was eager to preside over an official unveiling with press and TV coverage, the way the NIH publicity department preferred to make major announcements.

Red and yellow leaves blew down the street. The sky was a flawless clear blue. It was the kind of autumn day he and Robyn had loved when they came to Washington DC from Montreal two years earlier.

Matt recognized a woman from the endocrinology group coming toward him. She held her coat closed with one hand while trying to keep her hair from flying in the wind with the other. "Hi Carol," Matt greeted her. "Windy day. Do you know where Nakamishi is?"

"Poor man," she said continuing past Matt. "I heard he suffered a stroke yesterday."

Matt turned and caught back up with her, "Where is he now?"

"I think they took him to Georgetown Hospital."

Matt headed for the nearest Metro station.

• • •

"Mr. Nakamishi's impairment is severe," The doctor told Matt. "The stroke has damaged motor nerves on his left side, his speech center. There's significant cognitive impairment." The young doctor closed the folder. "We'll likely never know the proximate cause of his stroke. There is no obvious precursor; cholesterol levels were not elevated. He is fifty years old, non-smoking, not overweight, blood numbers near perfect." The doctor stood and shook hands with Matt. "I'm sorry there was so little we could do for your colleague."

They had not been close friends, but in the two years they had worked together on the micro-electronic-machine project, Matt had come to like the soft-spoken Nakamishi. The few times they went to the Dubliner bar across the street for beers after work, Nakamishi became jovial after his second Sam Adams. His face bright red, he would laugh himself into tears at every joke. But at nine o'clock sharp he'd gather up his things, pay his share of the tab, and excuse himself with the same set speech: "Time to go home. Very enjoyable tonight, thank you."

Nakamishi's eyes were open as Matt approached his bed. Eventually they focused. He brought his left hand out from under the sheet, fingers curled except thumb and little finger. His elbow rotated until his hand was at his left ear. His mouth trembled, trying to form words.

"I'm not sure what you mean," Matt said, unable to decipher what Nakamishi was so desperately trying to tell him. Nakamishi's forearm fell back onto the sheet and his eyes closed. Then he rallied, and with a trembling hand traced the letter "S" on the bedsheet before he sank back into semi-consciousness.

Lacking any better idea of where to go, Matt returned to his O street townhouse. He stood at the upstairs window watching autumn leaves rain down onto the cobbled sidewalk.

Nakamishi's paper was supposedly still in review. But it had been a week. If it truly was a breakthrough, NIH's publicity department should have been blaring the news already.

"Very strange." He located a mailer in his desk, addressed it to Robyn's parents in Montreal, and slipped the external drive inside. Then he paused. *No. Don't want to get her involved until I talk to her.*

"Why not go there?" he said aloud as the idea dawned on him. "She can get this mem design into the hands of the researchers at McGill University."

A minute change in sound, a wisp of cool air told Matt someone had opened the door downstairs.

Quick, loud footsteps on the stair, more than one person coming fast. As Matt turned to run, two men grabbed him from behind and threw him to the floor. The external drive flew out of his hand and under the bed. A young man with the look of a street punk knelt on Matt's chest and put a gun in his face.

"Shut up. Do as we say."

The two thugs marched Matt out of the house and shoved him into the back seat of a van, sandwiching him between them. The van drove onto I-395, westbound toward Virginia.

The man in the front passenger seat turned to face Matt. It was Mr. Sinqueford.

He nodded pleasantly. Suddenly, Matt felt the sting of a syringe. All volition drained out of him. He lost consciousness before they reached the Roosevelt Bridge.

When Matt woke, he was lying fully dressed on a comfortable bed in a colonial style bedroom. It could have been one of the stylish bed and breakfasts in Northern Virginia horse country. A Seth Thomas clock on a table across the room said three-fifteen. Through the lace sheers he could see a wide lawn and beyond that, a tree-covered hillside, brilliant in red and orange leaves.

He found the door locked, then sat on the bed trying to determine what to do. His head was foggy; every motion demanded great effort.

Presently, Sinqueford walked in and closed the door behind him.

"What the Hell is going on?" Matt demanded, but his voice was unsteady, his mouth full of cotton.

Sinqueford smiled. "It's a little chilly outside, but I find walking delightful this time of year. I'll explain as we walk." He handed Matt a brightly colored ski jacket, then donned a similar one. They strolled down a graveled path along a manicured slope of lawn between wide-spaced red oaks. The wind and sun felt enormously cheering.

The scarlet trees and green hills lay before them under a crystalline sky. "This lovely campus was built as a girl's school in the last century," Sinqueford said pleasantly. "In the 1950's the Defense Department took it over for a bacteriological warfare research facility." He chuckled. "Back in the days when we thought wars could be won with newer and better weapons." He laughed out loud. "Now we operate it."

"And who the hell are you anyway?" Matt growled. "Why have you kidnapped me and why did you attack Nakamishi?"

"We needed the mem design kept secret and kept in our hands, not made public," Sinqueford said evenly. He turned a concerned look on Matt. "You're feeling a little peaked, I presume. Marvelous drug, Midazolan, sometimes called Versed. Truth serum with the advantageous side effect of amnesia. You'll remember nothing of what you've told us, nor will you remember this conversation an hour from now." Sinqueford laughed. "Versatile Versed. Larger doses are used for lethal injections in prison executions in Florida and Ohio, I'm told. Which points up Mr. Nakamishi's concern about mems. Even the most benign tool can be weaponized if one has the imagination to do it. Mr. Nakamishi was becoming difficult about that point."

Soon they were back at the house, seated in a comfortable study. Two pairs of French doors overlooked the manicured lawn. "Your colleague Mr. Nakamishi," Sinqueford said slowly, "had that very counterproductive attribute—a conscience. In the weapons industry that is a great liability. He was threatening to destroy the design. He realized that our little microscopic platelets could be loaded with toxin as easily as they could be loaded with medicine."

"Who are you? Who do you work for? The Department of Defense?"

"No, you must be a U.S. citizen to work there," Sinqueford said.

"Then who do you work for?"

"NIH, of course. You are much like your friend Nakamishi aren't you? Smart, hard-working, idealistic, but so very blind to the ways of the world. Canadian, therefore able to distance your self from the stupidities of the Americans, while still living fully in the wealth and comfort they have created for all of us."

The study was warm. Outside, cloud shadows moved quickly over the hills. The wind rattled the French doors and moved the drapes with ghostly fingers.

"You'll remember none of this," Sinqueford told Matt. "I reveal all this for my own amusement. I am waiting for the drugs in your system to dissipate so we can deliver you home. All the drugs will dissipate, save one. The toxin-loaded mems we injected you with are the same ones we used on the unfortunate Nakamishi."

Matt froze.

The professor seemed pleased with himself, almost jovial. Matt sat dazed, unable to think clearly, both fearful and drowsy in the over-warm room.

"I am very grateful to the unfortunate Nakamishi," Sinqueford continued. "He developed an effective weapon, using American money and research facilities. We now have the design which we can keep secret, sell to the Israelis. The Israelis wanted a demonstration of the weapon, and Nakamishi provided an ideal subject. We injected him with toxin-loaded mems, he suffered a debilitating stroke, the weapon's effectiveness is proven and the Israelis send us their money. At the same time I am rid of a potential troublemaker whose conscience might have led him to tell the media about how our device can be weaponized. Now only you know about our little toys."

Matt's mind raced but he could think of no escape, no way to extricate himself. Sinqueford chuckled, "You should see the expression on your face. Fear not, we won't kill you. We need you, to continue your design work. But we must insist you remain loyal and silent."

Matt sat silent, trying to absorb all that had happened. Sinqueford glanced at his watch.

"As the Nazis taught the world, the best lie is a big lie. AIPAC, the Israeli lobby, is the best-funded lobbying group in Washington. They have sold the big lie that Islam is America's enemy. They profit from America's endless wars in the middle-east, and they shout 'anti-semite' at anyone who raises a voice against that strategy."

He shrugged. "No matter. You work for us now." He put his face close to Matt's. "Those mems will never leave your bloodstream. No doctor you consult will be able to detect them, but they are there. Anytime we feel you are … disloyal … we can send a signal to your phone, through your TV, through a metal detector you may walk through. There are a hundred ways to signal the mems to open their toxin cells."

He pulled his rotund face back, "Not worth taking a chance, is it? So, keep your mouth shut, continue working for us, and everything will be fine."

Sinqueford heaved himself to his feet. "Besides, we're the good guys. The Islamic nations are the enemy, right?"

Matt followed Sinqueford down a carpeted corridor to the front door. Fast moving low clouds had darkened the day. A cold wind skittered leaves across the flagstone patio and whirled them into piles along the low stone walls.

"Well, then," Sinqueford said, "I'll say goodbye.

For now."

Matt went down the stone steps on wobbly legs and got into the white van that had brought him.

From the door Sinqueford called, "Go back to your job. You're good at it, and we pay you well, don't we? Life is good."

In a rusty voice Matt called "You're blackmailing me. This is . . . " He could not find the words.

"It's not fair, is it?" Sinqueford said. "But then again, the world is not always fair, is it? But you are safe as long as you are loyal. We would be stupid to kill one of our best designers," Sinqueford laughed.

"Loyalty based on coercion..." Matt shouted.

"...is still loyalty," Sinqueford said. He raised a hand in farewell, "Think of us whenever you put a phone to your ear."

The van dropped Matt at his townhouse and sped away. He went inside and hurriedly began to pack his suitcase, then stopped. The Israelis would have him under surveillance. He stood motionless for a moment, then remembered the external drive. He reached under the bed. There it was. He slipped it into his pocket, pulled on his coat, and got into his car. He drove to the grocery store at the corner of 10th street.

He sat in the car a long time watching the flow of

vehicles and people, but he could detect no indication he was being followed.

If Nakamishi deleted all files before Sinqueford attacked him, I may have the only copy of the full design, Matt thought. Sinqueford has picked Nakamishi's brain and mine, so he knows the concepts and he's got some working models his stooges stole from the lab, but he would have to have another lab reverse engineer the mems to develop a design he could manufacture. "And that's what he expects me to do."

He started his car, drove out of DC and turned North on I-95. I should be able to cross the border into Canada before they can stop me. Get to McGill, find Robyn, and tell her and her colleagues about the weaponized mems. Publicize it before Israel can start manufacturing them in quantity. Develop a defense.

Matt threw his cell phone out the window as he accelerated.

Kasemba Coup

Oil industry consultant Martin Gibson is commissioned by the Economic Minister of Kasemba to buy a Russian warship to protect the country's offshore oil. But Martin soon learns he is only a pawn in an entirely unexpected power play.

Martin Gibson had just arrived in his office when the phone rang and the secretary informed him, "A Mr. Edward Mwanza calling from Poitre, Kasemba."

Martin watched the rain falling on London traffic for a moment, then pushed the lighted button, and Edward's mellifluous voice said in lightly accented English, "Hello, Martin?"

"Edward, old friend," Martin replied more heartily than he felt. "I'm pleased to hear from you. It's been a long time." They chatted for a bit about their student days twenty years before at the London School of Economics.

"Yesterday you sent me a substantial sum of money," Martin essayed. "Twenty million pounds."

"Yes. I need to impose on our friendship and ask you to handle a transaction for me."

Martin thought, *I'm not sure I want to launder funds for another third world leader fleeing with the nation's treasury.* "What do you have in mind, Edward?"

There was a smooth laugh at the other end of the line. "I know what you are thinking. 'Economic Minister flees Kasemba with state treasury,' but it is not that at all."

Martin relaxed a little.

"I know you will soon fly to eastern Russia—Vladivostok," Edward told Martin. "To assist Exxon-Mobil with their oil interests on Sakhalin Island." Martin was impressed. He had assumed that negotiating the third extension of Exxon-Mobil's oil extraction lease in eastern Russia was not a newsworthy item.

"What I would like for you to do with the money I sent you is to buy a small warship for Kasemba while you are in Vladivostok. Also a Russian crew that can be trusted. Instruct them to bring the ship to Poitre to protect Exxon-Mobil's oil platform that may be at risk from subversives. You have contacts in Vladivostok.

And your fee for handling the transaction would be one hundred thousand pounds."

Martin thought quickly. "My contacts in Vladivostok are oil industry people, not arms…"

"Would an increase in your fee to two hundred thousand pounds enable you to spend the time to find the people we need?"

Martin tilted back in his chair and watched rain speckle the window. "Well," he said at last, "Vlad is a small city; almost all the Russians there worked in the Navy yard when it was the headquarters of the Soviet Pacific Fleet. There may be a way."

"Excellent! It should not be too difficult. Warships are being sold as we speak," Edward said. "I know the South Africans and the Indians have recently bought warships there."

Martin hung up the phone, wondering if this was a good idea.

• • •

A thousand miles south of London, in the air-conditioned bar overlooking Le Meridien Hotel's swimming pool and the blue waters of Poitre Bay, Edward Mwanza watched Ari, the fat mercenary, clump up the stairs wearing gaudy pool attire. Edward's bodyguards at the next table muttered;

Edward raised the fingers of his hand, and they fell silent.

Edward stood as Ari approached. They shook hands, Edward masking his contempt behind an impassive look. He had mastered that look during his days as a student at the London School of Economics, during a time when black skin was still stared at on London streets.

Ari ordered an Amstel beer. Edward explained the mission to him. At the end of their conversation, one of Edward's men handed Ari a black briefcase. "You'll get the other half when the mission is complete," Edward apprised him. "No witnesses. Understand?"

Ari nodded.

• • •

It was spring in Vladivostok, but at night there was still frost. "Join me for a drink?" Yev, the Russian government negotiator, asked Martin as he pulled on his coat.

Martin shook his head. "No, I need to review these documents." They had spent several hours negotiating the definition of terms for the Exxon-Mobil oil exploration lease on 600,000 hectares of government-owned land on Sakhalin Island. Two stacks of paper lay on the table, each about ten centimeters high—

the negotiating position of the oil company, and the negotiating position of the Russian government.

"I'll tell you what," Yev said in Americanized English, "it's dinner time. Let's buy each other a drink, then I'll tell you what's in my documents and you tell me what's in yours, and we will agree on something in between. Then we can have a pleasant dinner, and neither one of us will have to read any of the documents."

Martin stuck out his hand. "Fair enough." He liked the Russian's breezy style.

They got into Yev's Toyota and drove to the harbor past surprisingly western-looking buildings, not a single Stalinist apartment block in sight. A four-lane street ran the length of the old Navy yard. "In the old days, nobody could drive along this street except us Pacific Navy people," Yev said to Martin. "Even the Army had to get a permit. All this was restricted." He waved at the dark wharves and the rows of ships. "Now, nobody comes down here." He pointed up the dark cross streets they drove past. "All this used to be full of action—a hundred bars and strips clubs, open day and night..."

"And you knew all of them," Martin said.

Yev smiled. "That was then." He pulled into

a muddy parking lot. Inside, the restaurant was smoke-filled, noisy, and cheerful. Two tables full of old men with crew cuts kept up a loud, beer-fueled conversation with each other and with the four waitresses. Martin grinned; the place had same Formica feel of the restaurant just off Highway 99 in Bakersfield where he used to meet the Standard Oil rep twenty years ago. Yev signaled for two beers. "Drink first, then we'll eat curry rice. It's pretty good."

"No vodka? No cabbage soup?"

Yev shrugged. "That's the other Russia…" Two tall brown bottles of Korean beer arrived. Yev poured, and they toasted each other and drank. By the time they had finished their curry rice, they'd reached a preliminary agreement on the Sakhalin oil and gas exploration option. They ordered more beer. Dinnertime was ending, but nobody had left the restaurant. Tall brown beer bottles with gold labels were filling the tables.

"Are you and I the only people who have to work tomorrow?" Martin asked, already feeling the effect of beer on top of jet lag.

Yev made a sad face. "Much unemployment in Vlad since the Navy yard closed."

"I would have thought people would've moved to

Moscow by now. Economy's booming there."

"Russians from west of the Urals are outsiders in Moscow. In Moscow you have to have connections. And besides, people from Vlad don't want to leave home. If we can get foreign investors in, and keep Moscow gangsters out, our economy will take off. We've got a lot of folks with manufacturing skills, and the Japanese and Chinese markets are close. This oil deal will help."

Yev smiled and poured Martin's glass full again. "I shouldn't have said that. Makes it look like we badly want the Exxon deal."

"Nothing wrong with being honest," Martin said. "You *should* want the Exxon-Mobil deal. It's good for you folks and good for the company. If these guys have skills, they can get work—pipelines, drill rigs, even the packaged mini-refineries."

"Skills?" Yev waved at the crowd of men sitting at bottle-littered tables behind him. "Everybody in Vlad used to work for the shipyard, one way or another—machinists, pipefitters, welders, logistics…every industrial skill."

Martin grew thoughtful. "In the meantime, would you consider some consulting work?"

"For Exxon-Mobil?"

"No, for an independent client. I've been approached by a client for some help on a business deal that I think might interest you."

Yev looked pensive. "Well...to tell you the truth Martin, my knowledge of the oil and gas business is actually pretty thin..."

"I could tell when we were negotiating."

"How bad a deal did I get?"

"You got a good deal. Exxon-Mobil isn't out to cut bad deals. And they don't need your knowledge of the oil business; they need your connections to local political and labor organizations. They need access to the local power structure at a level that is reliable and stable. Oil companies lose more from local government incompetence and corruption than from bad terms in the contract. They're eager to offer generous terms if they can find someone trustworthy enough to stick with the deal. Believe me, I know. Over the years, I've represented all the major oil firms in half a dozen countries."

"What's this other deal you have for me?" Yev asked.

"Kasemba. A small country in West Africa where Exxon-Mobil is about to start pumping oil. It's just getting underway. One offshore well right now, right out in the bay opposite Poitre City, the capital. In addition to ship loading facilities on the platform, Exxon-Mobil has installed a pipeline inland two kilometers where they will install a packaged mini-refinery to make refined product—car gas and truck diesel. Once oil starts flowing, the income will grow Kasemba's economy at ten times its present rate."

"So what's the problem?" Yev asked. "Sounds like a good thing for Kasemba. I wish we had oil here."

"Terrorism," Martin said softly. "The second biggest problem oil companies face in the third world is terrorists blowing up the infrastructure. These terrorists are usually tribal groups who feel the government has excluded them from the oil income. Which is often true—the king keeps all the oil income and the people get nothing." Martin waved his hands. "Anyway, my client, the government of Kasemba, needs a ship to protect the oil platform. The Economic Development Minister sent me here to buy a diesel submarine."

"Submarine," Yev said. He raised his glass, noticed it was empty, set it back down very deliberately. He pulled a roll of rubles from his pocket and left some on the table. "Let's walk. No wind tonight; it's not too cold."

There was no traffic, so they walked down the

middle of the cracked concrete street to a guardhouse at one of the entrances to the Navy yard. Yev had a short, jovial conversation in Russian with the guard on duty. "An old friend," he told Martin. He turned on a large black flashlight and led Martin down the wide concrete wharf between two rows of silent black submarines.

Yev flashed a light on the mast numbers as they passed. "This one, one of the best of the diesel boats. Her captain was a classmate of mine. He kept his ship well maintained. Let's go aboard."

They crossed the catwalk and went in a forward hatch. The inside was cold and dank, smelling of diesel fuel and oil, rust and saltwater. But Martin was surprised at how clean and orderly it was.

"Usually some of the electrical stuff is gone, sold," Yev said. "And sometimes the engine controls and the fuel injectors on the diesels, but we don't just torch them off. Our guys do it right; they unbolt, disconnect...let's take a look." They went down the narrow corridor to the engine room. The twin diesels looked clean and maintained. "Our fathers and our uncles built these boats," Yev said softly. They went to the wardroom and Yev propped the light on the polished teak tabletop. "Those guys back in the restaurant spent their careers working in this Navy yard, maintaining these boats. They like to stay near them. They feel like they own them." He frowned at the tabletop. "But times change. Now, everything is for sale."

There was a painting of a birch forest and snow-covered mountains on one bulkhead. "Are the maintenance logs available?" Martin asked.

"Sure," Yev said. "But they will do you no good. Those entries were made for the political officers and the bureaucrats at Navy headquarters in Moscow. Very high-quality fiction." He shook his head. "You and your client will have to take our word that these boats are reliable. Our fathers built these boats; we maintained them." Yev touched his head. "Our records are here."

"Any crewmembers still around?"

"Some. The young conscripts have all gone home, but some of the old petty officers are still around."

"Think a skeleton crew could be hired? Experienced men?"

Yev shrugged. It was silent in the boat, like a ghostly cave.

"Depends on the mission." He looked at Martin. "Weapons guys might be hard to find…but men who know the boats and can run them…they're still here. The South Africans have bought four of these boats, and the Indians are bargaining now. The problem will be to procure arms, torpedoes. You should talk to the Israelis about that stuff."

"My client already has. You are to pick a boat, get it running, fuel it, and take it to Pointe Noir, Congo Empire. It's a corrupt country—the port is wide open, bribes have already been paid," Martin informed Yev. "An Israeli weapons man will meet you there and oversee loading munitions. Then you run up the coast to Poitre Bay. It should be about a ten hour run on the surface."

Yev considered this for a long time. "How much? For the boat, fuel, and four men?"

"Fifteen million US?"

The underwater noises of the harbor entered the cold steel cylinder of the submarine—soft groans and rattles. Phantoms moving in the blackness outside the hull.

"We will need more," Yev said slowly.

"Eighteen million," Martin said.

Yev said nothing for a moment. Then, "How long do we stay in Kasemba? Maybe one day?"

"As long as it takes to train a local crew."

Yev laughed long and loud. "Train a local crew?"

"Shouldn't take you more than two weeks," Martin guessed. "All the Kasemba Navy has to do is cruise around the bay making sure no terrorists in surface craft get near the oil platform. Submerge once in a while so the bad guys don't know where they are. Then surface and stand guard. The sub won't be armed with torpedoes, only machine guns on the deck. Maybe some surface-to-surface shoulder-launched missiles. The Israeli mercenary has been hired to bring all that stuff. You just get a sub running, bring it to West Africa, and train a local crew to operate it."

Yev laughed again. "This crew, even after we train them, I'm sure they will submerge with hatches open and sink their own boat." He laughed again, a long ringing laugh.

Martin stood. "I need to take a piss."

He and Yev stood side by side on the concrete wharf pissing into the black water between two subs. "If the Kasemba Navy sinks their own boat, that is not your problem," Martin said. His breath blew clouds of steam at the stars. "Do your training quickly, then get out of Kasemba before you are blamed for something. Two weeks maximum."

"I am pissing a toast," Yev said. "A toast to the Kasemba Navy."

"I'll buy you and your men a drink at the Meridien Hotel bar in Poitre City when you've delivered the boat and completed the training," Martin told him. "I've been invited to the ribbon cutting ceremony for the oil platform."

They walked down the long concrete wharf past the row of black submarines. Martin fished in his jacket pocket and handed Yev a cell phone. If you need to contact me in Kasemba, call me on this phone. Phone service in Kasemba is not reliable."

Yev and Martin passed through the security gate, and Yev drove Martin to his hotel.

"I have an early flight," Martin said, "so I won't see you again until we meet in Kasemba. Good luck." They shook hands. Yev's face was somber in the starlight.

• • •

The Russians sat in the shade of the submarine's mast, sweltering in the tropical heat of Pointe Noir. A hot wind blew off the dirty green water of the harbor. The Israeli was late. Yev checked his watch for the third time.

"This could be him," Markov said, shading his eyes against the glare. Two Mercedes trucks were coming up the gravel road to the dock. In the dust cloud behind them, a mobile crane rumbled along.

Yev disliked the fat Israeli the moment he stepped down from the truck, a heavy backpack in his hand.

"You're Yevtushenko?" he said in English, looking at Markov.

Yev stepped forward. "I'm Yev. You're Ari?"

The mercenary nodded.

"Then let's get to work," Yev said, "so we can get out of here tonight."

The second truck had backed around to let the crane get close to the dock and the sub. The crane was extending its outriggers while a crew of black men, mostly teenagers, was slinging three-meter lengths of black steel angle out of the truck with an unholy racket. Another group unhitched a Miller welding unit from the back of the second truck and jockeyed it up to the edge of the dock. It was apparently stolen from Shell Oil Pipeline Division. The decals were still on it.

"First we cut to length, then we weld," Ari told Yev in English.

"What welding?" Yev snapped. "No welding on my boat." Ari stiffened.

Several black Africans in ragtag clothes walked across the board catwalk to the sub's afterdeck. With a tape measure, they began making chalk marks on the raised deck tracks.

"Rocket launcher base," Ari said shortly, and he turned to yell something at the men with the measuring tape.

"No welding on the hull of my boat," Yev told the Israeli.

"They are welding onto the deck lattice, not hull," Ari said. "And this is not your boat." He turned away to supervise the work.

Yev and the crew retreated to a nearby warehouse office, where a laboring window air conditioner provided some relief. Markov and the other crewmen watched out the dirty window, muttering in Russian and shaking their heads.

After a canted steel frame had been assembled and mounted on the sub's afterdeck, the crane lifted two Exocet air-to-ship missile launch tubes onto the framework, and Ari personally oversaw the attachment of the tubes to the frame.

Ari came into the office drenched with sweat, still carrying his backpack. "Eight hours surface running time to Poitre Bay?" he asked.

"Yes," Yev said.

"I pay my people, then let's go." He went out into the heat.

Yev and his crew crossed to the boat while Ari doled out US dollars to the welders, the truck drivers, the laborers, and the crane operator, and the workmen sped away. Then Ari went to the two overweight black men in tennis shoes lounging in the warehouse shade beside their AK-47s. He unrolled some money for them too, then came aboard the sub and slid the walkway board back onto the dock. "Let's go."

Yev tilted his head at Markov. "Let's go," he said in Russian.

• • •

Soon they were running at ten knots on the surface. Markov kept front and rear hatches open to let the humid sea breeze blow through the interior of the boat. Slowly the color of the ocean was changing from green to blue.

Evening came. Yev took a final sun sight at sunset and plotted their position. They'd made good progress up the coast, and were within Kasemba's territorial waters already. No reefs between Pointe Noir and Poitre Bay, and the lights of the city would give them some reference points.

"All surface running," Markov said quietly to Yev. They stood shoulder to shoulder in the cramped conning tower opening, the sea breeze in their faces. "Can't submerge with that." Markov thrust his chin at the two missile tubes in their steel lattice frames. "I don't like not being able to submerge."

"Neither do I. It's not what the Brit told me when I agreed to this deal, but…we get the sub to Poitre Bay, to the oil platform, then we leave. I will tell them they can hire mercenaries to train their crew to run this boat."

• • •

They reached Poitre Bay an hour before dawn. Coming into the bay, the wind had shifted, bringing the land scents of equatorial Africa. Using binoculars, Yev scanned Poitre Bay from the bright lights of the presidential palace at one end to the airport at the other. Markov studied the oil terminal in the middle of the bay. It was gleaming with construction lights.

Ari came out on the aft deck carrying his ever-present backpack. He opened a panel on one of the missile tubes and peered into the compartment with a flashlight. He made some adjustments, closed the panel, then moved to the second missile.

"Now what?" Markov asked Yev.

"We wait for dawn, then come alongside the oil platform," Yev said. The bay was dead calm. With the engines stopped, the only sounds were Ari's clicking and probing in the second missile.

• • •

Markov squatted down out of earshot of Ari. Yev did the same, got a Marlboro going, and offered one to Markov. "Ari is not to be trusted…"

Markov touched his left side, a gesture indicating a gun. "Maybe we should eliminate him. He won't be missed."

"Not in our contract. Besides, the Brit needs him to train the locals to use those missiles." Yev blew smoke. "Missiles. I don't understand why missiles."

There was a loud splash. Yev peered over the steel wall. The lights of Poitre City twinkled in the humid night air. Ari was no longer on deck, but was in the water. A rubber raft was inflating. A two-cycle engine whined to life, and Ari sped away from the sub on his little boat.

Yev and Markov stared after him as he disappeared into darkness.

• • •

Suddenly, the first missile ignited with a coughing roar and screamed off the launch platform in a plume of red and yellow flame. The second one followed. As the smoke cleared, the two Russians watched the missiles curve around, skimming the surface of the water and aiming straight for the lights of the oil platform.

Yev cursed in Russian. In less than thirty seconds, the two red sparks of light merged with the glittering lights of the oil terminal. An orange-red fireball bloomed and rolled skyward. The Russians watched a compression wave race across the still water of the bay and lap over the hull. The sound of the shock wave reached them a second later.

The oil platform began to cant slowly down on one side. There was another double concussion. The platform canted further and separated into two segments, one falling into the ocean, the other one twisting and settling into a tangle of steel at the water's surface. Black smoke boiled up into a sky just going gray with the coming dawn. The helipad broke free and fell onto one of the boats moored under the platform.

"Get below," Yev said. "We get out of here!" The sub's engines started as Yev stormed into the control room. "Hard aport, full power. Get us out of here!"

Markov took his place at the dive controls. The

crew had the sub underway again, turning in a wide sweep toward the open ocean.

"Steer 260," Yev directed the steersman. That's when Yev saw the charges taped to the bottom of the control panels. "Now what has he done?" Yev growled.

He stooped to examine the olive green blocks of explosive taped to the underside of the control panels. There was an igniter set in each one. Yev knew if he pulled it out, the charges would go off.

He pulled the steersman bodily out of his seat and screamed, "Get out of the boat! There is a bomb!" Yev shouted down the length of the boat, "Get out! There is a bomb!"

Men scrambled up the ladder and onto the deck. Yev followed them up. "Get overboard! Get away from the boat! It's going to blow up." He shoved two men down the round flank of the sub and into the water. "Swim!"

Markov hesitated.

"Go!" Yev screamed. He shoved Markov in, then jumped after him, scraping over barnacles on the hull as he slid. Once in the water, he swam as hard as he could away from the sub.

The sub glided away toward the dark horizon.

From water level it seemed to be moving very fast. Then there was a blast and the thump of a shock wave in the water. The sub heaved up and rolled to port. In less than a minute, it was gone.

Yev treaded water slowly. The water was warm.

"Now what?" Markov coughed.

"Everybody make it out?" Yev asked. Voices grunted. "Now we swim. To the side of the bay with no lights." The oil platform was still burning, red and gray reflections on the bay in the breaking dawn.

Two hours later, the tide deposited the six Russians on the beach near a shantytown a long way from the city. A few rotted wooden fishing boats were pulled up on the sand. In their shade, a couple of black kids in filthy shorts eyed them, but kept their distance.

Yev lay exhausted. He was burning with thirst and so tired he couldn't move his arms. Markov got to his knees and crawled over to him.

"You OK?"

"Yeah." Yev struggled to a sitting position.

"You still got your wallet?" Markov asked. "Mine's gone."

Yev touched his pants pocket. His soggy wallet was still there. And the phone Martin had given him. Yev had put it in a waterproof bag to keep the constant moisture in the boat out of it.

"Any money?"

Yev thought for a moment. "About a hundred US dollars, and some rubles. Why?"

"'Cause you're buying drinks for us at the poolside bar at the Intercontinental," Markov said straight-faced. Yev laughed. "A pirate's life, yes?"

Yev snorted. "I don't think we'd be very welcome at any hotel in this town."

After a while, they got to their feet and struggled to a ragged store in the middle of the shantytown. The attendant, an old black woman, brought them bottles of warm cola. She didn't seem very curious why six foreigners would be swimming in the ocean with their clothes on.

"You oil man?" she said in English. She glanced toward the smoke still rising from the remains of the oil terminal. "When we get oil money?"

Yev pulled out the phone Martin had given him in Vladivostok, and pushed the callback number. The old woman disappeared into the back of the ramshackle store.

• • •

Martin had first class to himself on the night flight from London to Paris. But on his connecting flight to Poitre City at Charles de Gaulle Airport, all the seats around him filled up. Wide Kasemban women festooned with Harrods shopping bags engaged in lively conversation. Martin tried to keep his attention on his review of Kasemba's economic data, but it was hard with people going up and down the aisles and women chattering all around him.

Noting several international news teams on board, he asked one of the Reuters people why there were so many news people going to Kasemba.

"President Mwanza is doing a ribbon cutting at a big new lumber mill," the guy said to Martin. "Don't know why that's news, but my boss said go and I go."

"Lumber mill or oil terminal?" Martin asked.

The Reuters guy put his *Paris Match* aside and switched off his overhead light. "Told me a lumber mill, but could be oil, don't know."

The plane landed at 5 AM, and Martin filed off with the other yawning passengers. After the usual slow lines at customs and immigration, Martin went out into the cool predawn air and caught the last available taxi before the news teams cleared customs.

"Meridien Hotel, please," Martin told the driver,

and they set off at a snail's pace down the highway to the city. Martin rolled his window down and let the earthy scents of Africa roll over him. His room on the fifth floor of the Meridien Hotel had bad soap and only one threadbare towel, but the bed felt comfortable and the air conditioning worked. He opened the drapes wide to a dawn view of Poitre Bay, with Exxon-Mobil's oil platform a glittering jewel in the placid water. He slid his glass door open to the cool morning air.

Martin's appointment with Economic Minister Edward Mwanza was not until nine o'clock, which would give him time to take a shower and change clothes. He was just turning away when he happened to notice two sparks of light just above the surface of the bay. They made a long curve, nearly a half circle, growing closer and accelerating straight at the oil platform.

Frozen with disbelief, Martin stood watching the two missiles hit the platform and explode in a giant fireball. A moment later the sound wave rattled the sliding glass doors. Smoke was rising to the sky. A part of the platform broke off and fell into the bay.

A babble of voices rose up from the swimming pool terrace as a crowd of hotel employees rushed to the wall separating the pool terrace from the beach.

They were pointing and squawking at each other.

Martin went down the stairs to the lobby bar. The bartender was nowhere in sight so Martin snagged a bottle of gin and some tonic and removed himself to a safe corner while people ran this way and that. Nearly two hours later, Martin's second cell phone rang. He clawed it out of his briefcase. It was Yev. "What's going on?" Martin asked, trying to keep his voice down.

"Your mercenary fired missiles at platform, then sank the sub."

"Where are you?"

"By the beach. We all got out alive, but the Israeli escaped. I don't know where he…"

"Where are you right now?" Martin said urgently. There was a pause. Martin checked his watch—seven-thirty, and Edward's limo was to pick him up at nine.

"Some shantytown around the bay on the beach; woman here says 'Arenta.' "

"Stay where you are," Martin said. "I'll get a taxi, come and get you." He clicked off, went upstairs and got his briefcase, then back out to the taxi stand in front of the hotel.

Four empty taxis were there, their drivers jabbering and pointing at the burning oil platform.

"I need to get to Arenta right now," Martin told the first driver. He pulled out a 100 Euro note and shoved it into the man's hand. "Fast! OK?"

The driver glanced at his colleagues, then jumped in the aged Toyota, and they drove off in a blast of exhaust smoke.

• • •

"You owe us more than one round of drinks for this mess," Yev told Martin when he showed up at the shantytown store twenty minutes later. But Martin was not laughing.

Martin pressed a packet of British hundred pound notes into Yev's hand. "Get out of Kasemba fast!" Martin glanced around. "If the local forces find you, they'll convict you of terrorism and execute you. Take this money and go. I have to go. I'm supposed to meet the Economic Minister's car at the Meridien in less than an hour. Assuming the Army doesn't close the country down after this."

"Which way is the border?" Yev asked, suddenly serious.

"Down this road about five kilometers is the truck stop at the Exxon-Mobil pump station. There are always trucks there looking for cargo to haul. Pay a driver to take you to the Gabon border, which is about sixty kilometers farther down the road. Then bribe your way across, get to Libreville Airport, and take the first flight to Johannesburg. Everybody still got their passports?"

Yev translated and the Russians all held up their waterlogged passports. "Good," Martin said. "You can tell the immigration people at Libreville Airport your entrance visa was obscured when your boat sank. Tell them you work for Exxon-Mobil." Martin pulled out some generic Exxon information center business cards and passed them around. "These don't mean anything, but the airport people may accept your story if you show them these cards and slip them a bribe."

Martin jumped back in the waiting taxi and disappeared in cloud of dust.

The Russians started down the road the other direction at a fast walk.

• • •

The hotel was a madhouse of news crews and Kasemba military when Martin arrived. He went up to his room, showered, put on a clean suit, and was back downstairs in front of the hotel when his other phone rang and a woman told him that Mr. Edward

Mwanza would like to postpone their meeting one hour. A car would arrive for him at ten o'clock.

Martin went back into the empty hotel lobby. Outside, a huge crowd of foreign reporters had gathered around a cluster of Africans in business suits. Behind them on the beach, military men were patrolling, and a Caterpillar D7 with a sand drill had drilled six holes just above high tide. The sand drill was dropped off, and a side-arm loader attached to the dozer. Six short telephone poles were slipped into the holes. Army troops with shovels straightened the poles and filled sand around them.

• • •

Martin's blood chilled when he saw several men with black hoods over their heads and their hands tied behind their backs being marched out toward the poles. The foreign news teams had their cameras set up on the hotel terrace, getting the spectacle on video.

Martin turned away and paced through the empty lobby, trying to keep his mind clear, considering taking a taxi to the airport. But he knew the airport would be closed to outbound flights.

• • •

A volley of shots rattled the glass of the lobby. Soon afterward, people began making their way back inside. The foreigners demanded the bar be opened, and after conferring with the management, the accommodating black bartender started pouring. Martin wanted a drink himself, but instead paced the lobby nervously, checking his watch. It wasn't long until the hotel TVs were showing the executions. Six men, subversives, had been caught trying to escape after sabotaging Exxon-Mobil's oil platform. A military tribunal had tried and convicted them this morning.

The TV showed the six men tied to the poles set in the sand. A firing squad quickly disposed of them while TV cameras videoed the event, nicely backgrounded by the smoking ruin of the oil platform.

Martin looked at his watch. It had been exactly three hours since he'd witnessed the explosion. Outside, the bodies had already been removed and the dozer was pushing out the poles and leveling the beach. Soldiers were loading the poles on an army truck.

Martin watched in disgust as the hotel's tractor pulled a beach comb up and down the sand, smoothing the sand, covering the blood. Within a few moments, hotel staff members were setting up beach umbrellas and chairs. The bay sparkled blue under a tropical sun.

• • •

Foreign news teams crowded the bar. Government-owned TV-K for once was broadcasting foreign programs. Reporters and cameramen made bets in a dozen currencies as to whose coverage would break first. A cheer went up as Television Luxembourg broke into the *Alouette* series to show France-Union's coverage of the sabotage and executions in Kasemba. The newsmen finished their beers and hauled their luggage to the lobby, where taxis were waiting to take them to the airport. The TV was soon turned off as government programming resumed.

• • •

Martin was standing in front of the hotel's glass doors when Edward, in the armored presidential Mercedes limo, its windows jet black, idled up the hotel's circle drive. Martin climbed into the frigid air conditioning. Edward, dressed in a bespoke blue pinstripe suit, sat impassive in the wide leather seat. They rode to the airport in silence. Soldiers with AK-47s stood guard at the airport entrances. Martin collected his briefcase and stepped out of the car into tropical heat.

The power window of the limousine slid down.

"It's better this way, Martin…" Edward said calmly.

Martin was already beginning to sweat in the morning heat. "I don't like being lied to and being used in this way, Edward. You made me the middleman in your decision to blow up Exxon-Mobil's platform. Many people died, Edward. I thought you were a better man than that. And, conveniently, you had foreign news people here to cover your staged execution of some poor nobodies 'convicted' of blowing up the oil platform!" Comprehension dawned on Martin suddenly. "Your brother was among those executed, wasn't he?"

Edward's face had an impenetrable look. "The news people are here to cover the opening of a lumber mill today. Wood has always been our largest foreign currency export, and it will continue to be, now that the oil will stay in the ground for a few more years. The wood industry is not dominated by such powerful companies as the oil industry is."

"You had your own brother executed on the beach this morning." Martin's voice was shaking with fury. "You maneuvered me into bringing money to the Russians to buy a boat to blow up the oil platform. I will go to the international courts in The Hague, and to Exxon-Mobil..."

"That would be ill-advised, Martin," Edward said softly. "I have a video of you bringing money to the Russians in Vladivostok. The news media will believe whatever story sells best. And my story will be a very good story indeed: a consultant hired by a rival oil company, perhaps Shell Oil, is paid to buy a Russian sub to sabotage Exxon-Mobil...much investment is lost, many people die, a poor African nation loses the bright future that oil could have brought."

Martin regarded the impassive face before him. "I thought we respected each other more than that, Edward."

"My brother kept this country in chains, while he and his cronies lived very well. With oil income, they would have tightened their stranglehold on the people of Kasemba and enriched themselves even more. I am a force for change, Martin, but I must make that change happen more slowly, using traditional ways..."

"A dictator's ways..."

"A tribal leader's way. The oil must stay in the ground a few years longer. Give me time to build a middle class here in Kasemba," Edward said. "Find the right people at Exxon-Mobil. You are a respected consultant; they will listen to you. Convince them not to come back to Kasemba. Tell them to search for oil in Sao Tome, in Guinea-Bissau, in Cameroon. Talk to President Odimba in Gabon. But do not come to Kasemba."

The limousine's window slid up soundlessly, and the car pulled away.

• • •

That evening after the grand opening of the largest lumber processing plant in West Africa, President Edward Mwanza's limousine took him to the Liban restaurant. Ari was at a table near the balcony when Mwanza's bodyguards came in, cleared all other diners and staff out, and carefully searched each table and chair for bombs.

Ari finished his Amstel, and tried to find a waiter to order another one.

Mwanza entered accompanied by two bodyguards. One positioned himself at the front door, the other at the end of the balcony. Mwanza sat down opposite the Israeli. Ari craned around the empty room, searching for a waiter. Mwanza said something to a bodyguard in Bantu, and a nervous waiter brought an Amstel and quickly retired.

"Four hundred thousand sterling," Ari said after a

long drink from the bottle. "The platform is destroyed, the sub sunk, no accomplices, no witnesses."

Mwanza studied the other man's florid features as though trying to memorize them. He turned a little in the rattan chair and nodded at the bodyguard at the end of the balcony, who brought a black leather briefcase to the table and set it in front of Ari. Inside were packets of crisp British pound notes, denominated in hundreds. Ari hurriedly fanned each packet, then closed the case.

"I have a taxi outside for you," Mwanza said. "It will take you to the airport, where there is a ticket at the counter for you on the 10:30 Air Liban flight to Beirut."

Ari rose and made his way out the door of the silent restaurant. An ancient Mercedes 230 taxi was idling at the curb, back door and trunk open. As Ari passed by, the bodyguard at the door shot him neatly in the back of the head. Ari fell forward onto the pavement, his blood conveniently caught by the curb. One bodyguard retrieved the briefcase, and another put a check round into what was left of Ari's head. The two of them wrestled Ari's body into a body bag and into the trunk of the taxi, and drove away.

Inside, President Mwanza enjoyed a pleasant dinner.

www.ingramcontent.com/pod-product-compliance
Lightning Source LLC
Chambersburg PA
CBHW070937250626
47159CB00009B/3287